HOW TO SEDUCE A BAD BOY

A POINT BEACON NOVEL
BOOK 1

TRACI DOUGLASS

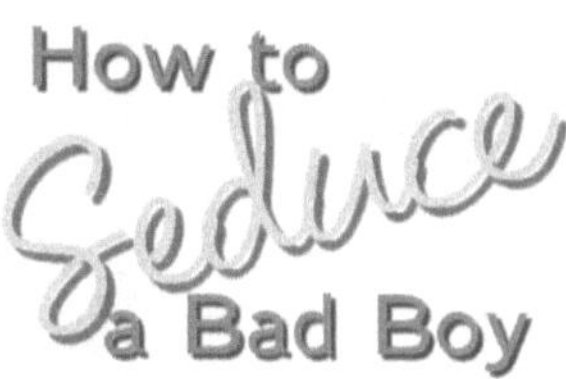

She's ready to break all the rules…

Librarian Melody Bryant loves order. Loves rules and deadlines. Loves books. But what she doesn't love is still being unattached at twenty-four. Unfortunately, the only guy she's ever crushed on turned her down flat. And then left town.

Now, with her birthday looming and a new promotion at work up for grabs, she just can't take it any longer. But she needs help to bust her good girl reputation and knows the perfect man for the job: Her former crush who's just as broodingly gorgeous and unavailable as before.

This Army vet won't know what hit him…

CHAPTER ONE

"Thanks for—" *Nothing*.

Melody Bryant barely had time to avoid getting her toes run over as her latest first date pulled away from the curb in a flurry of exhaust and squealing tires.

With a sigh, she trudged up the walkway to her quaint little bungalow on a quiet side street in Point Beacon, Indiana. She'd really thought this evening had been going well, too. Her date du jour had been Michael Bennett, owner of their tiny town's only buy-here, pay-here used car emporium and last year's winner of the Chamber of Commerce's top entrepreneur award. And yes, maybe he had been a bit...*smarmy*—in that aggressive salesman sort of way—with no regard for personal space or breath mints, but still.

Shoulders slumped, Mel unlocked her front door and pushed inside, her fluffy Birman cat darting over to twine around her ankles. She tossed her stuff on the side table in the foyer, then bent to scratch the purring feline behind the ears. "Another one bites the dust, eh, Waldo?"

Waldo meowed, as if in sympathy.

After toeing off her cute red-and-white Mary Jane pumps, she grabbed her cell phone from her purse, then padded down the short hall to the kitchen to grab the canister of M&M's she kept on her counter at all times.

Mel balanced the large glass container on one hip as she proceeded into her open-style living room and plopped into the corner of the overstuffed beige sofa. She pried open the lid of the canister with one hand while hitting speed dial for her best friend with the other, then began sorting the candy into the colors she liked—blue, red, and, most especially, green.

Lilly Martin answered on the second ring. "How'd it go?"

"Not good." Between popping candies into her mouth, Mel explained the events of her newest dating fail. "I mean, it started out fine. Dinner at Stubby's Steakhouse, talking about our jobs, our goals, our dreams for the future. Then, of course, he went into all his hot librarian fantasies."

"Ewww," Lilly said, her shudder evident through the phone line. "That's nasty."

"Hey, it's not like I haven't heard it before." She devoured another handful of M&M's, then parroted Mike's worst come-on. "You must have overdue books, honey, because you've got fine written all over you."

Lilly snorted. "Nice. How about, 'It's not the size of the collection, it's how you use it.'"

Mel giggled. "No, no. My all-time favorite was, 'Good thing I've got my library card, 'cause I'm totally checking you out.'"

They laughed so hard and long, Mel's stomach hurt by the

time she stopped. In the silence that followed, however, harsh reality returned. Given her lack of boyfriend and no prospects on the horizon at the ripe old age of twenty-four, she felt terminally boring and doomed to be stuck in the "friend zone" for eternity. "Seriously, though, what the heck am I missing here?"

Lilly sighed. "Besides a hot man in your bed?"

"Exactly." Mel straightened slightly to run the fingers of her free hand through Waldo's thick grayish-white fur. "Tell me where to find one of those super studs and I'll be all over him."

"Cool your jets there, Maverick." Lilly chuckled. "Have you stopped to consider maybe you're coming across too eager? Most guys like a challenge. Then there's the whole nightmare of your wardrobe."

"What's wrong with my wardrobe?" Mel scowled down at her calf-length red pencil skirt and cream-colored twinset. The pearls might be a bit much, but they'd belonged to her grandmother.

"Nothing, if you're ninety and your name's June Cleaver."

Mel slammed the lid back on the canister and set it on the coffee table. "I don't look like June Cleaver. I dress for comfort. Plus, it gets cold in the library, so I wear layers to keep warm."

"Good, because those cardigans are the *only* things that'll keep you toasty on the long winter nights ahead." Lilly's tone held a hint of pity, which set Mel's hackles rising. Her best friend had no room to talk. She went through men like tissues, never seeming to stay with one guy too long. Like Goldilocks, no one was just right—too short, too tall, too fat, too thin, talks too much, doesn't talk enough. Mel had begun to wonder if there was a man alive perfect enough for her best friend. Though there *had* been that one night, right before Mel's older brother, James, had left for basic training. She'd thought there might have been something between them, but Lilly had always denied it and James had since come out as gay, so... Anyway, this conversation was about Mel's romantic adventures, or lack thereof.

"Look," Lilly said, jarring Mel out of her thoughts. "All I'm saying is it wouldn't kill you to show a bit of skin, maybe play down the prim."

Arms crossed, Mel cradled the phone between her shoulder and ear. "I'm not prim, I'm classic. Besides, I don't want to be with a guy who only wants me if I pretend to be something I'm not."

"I'm not asking you to change who you are," Lilly said. "Just highlight your assets."

My assets? Mel glanced down at her ample bust and wide hips, then at the M&M's container beckoning her to finish it off. Lilly was right, darn it, and it was all so unfair. Her twenty-fifth birthday was coming up in a month—August 14, to be exact—and she was still a virgin.

Sure, maybe being a virgin in your mid-twenties wasn't exactly a predicament equivalent to say, a raging case of Ebola, but it felt pretty darned close to Mel. Especially tonight. Most likely, her lingering maidenhead was the reason for her recent bout of dating desperation—and the only sane excuse Mel could come up with for considering born-to-be-wild Lilly's advice.

After all, keeping it classy sure hadn't worked well in the love department thus far.

Honestly, Mel's problems with the men of Point Beacon had started clear back in high school. From the day she'd turned sixteen and her parents had finally allowed her to date, all the local guys thought she was too type A, too high maintenance, too "good girl."

Maybe that was true. She exhaled slowly and collapsed back against the couch cushions, feeling defeated. She ran the best dang library in central Indiana yet couldn't seem to make it past a first date. Let alone find a man to make all her wicked desires and fantasies come true.

It was frustrating. It was pitiful. It was ridiculous.

And it was all Adam Foster's fault.

Mel wouldn't be in this pristine mess now if her older brother's best friend had slept with her the night she'd propositioned him eight years ago. But no. Adam had to be all noble and heroic and tell her she was special and should wait for the right guy to come along.

"...and what you need to do is get rid of this good-girl image you've got looming over you like a shroud." Lilly's words jolted Mel back to the present. Perhaps her best friend was right. She'd been good until now. Maybe it was time to temper the sweet with a bit of spice.

It was bad enough her parents constantly hounded her these days about giving them grandkids. Now the townsfolk were chiming in, too. Today, for instance, she'd been walking home from work and old Gus MacMillan, the cantankerous owner of Point Beacon Hardware, had stopped sweeping his sidewalk to ask Mel when she was going to "get hitched and have babies."

Then again, he might've been trying to rile her up. She and Gus weren't on the best of terms lately since she'd chewed him out last week about getting his library card, then not using it.

Still, her reproductive activities, or lack thereof, were none of his business.

Mel sighed and closed her eyes, focusing on a solution.

What she needed was direction. An achievable course of action to lose her virginity by her twenty-fifth birthday—five short weeks from now.

In the end, she really only had one man in mind for the job.

A tall order, but not impossible, given that Adam was back in Point Beacon following two tours in the army. Mel had stopped by his body shop under the guise of scheduling maintenance for her car, to see if Adam still looked the same. He did— all tall, dark, and tantalizingly unavailable.

But he hadn't so much as glanced her way. Then she'd ended up missing her bogus appointment at his garage because of a delivery snafu at the library. She'd yet to speak one word to the guy since his return, even though he lived just down the road, but each night she'd hear the sound of his motorcycle, rumbling past her house after he got off work, and her knees went wobbly picturing gorgeous bad boy Adam with all that roaring power between his thighs.

"Uh, I need to go, Lils."

"Wait." Her best friend's tone grew suspicious. "What are you going to do?"

The familiar sound of a Harley-Davidson grew louder in the distance, and adrenaline swamped Mel's system, causing her heartrate to triple. Adam Foster was on his way home, and her future suddenly looked a whole lot brighter.

"I've got a plan. Talk to you later."

Mel ended the call without saying goodbye, tossed her phone on the coffee table, then headed down the hall toward her front door, doing a quick check of her reflection in the foyer mirror. Same petite figure. Same long dark brown hair. Same big green eyes. Tonight, though, her gaze sparkled with new determination. She wasn't the besotted, naive girl Adam had left behind eight years ago. Now she was a successful woman with a good job and a home of her own.

She was ready.

Or not.

She might've overstated the whole "having a plan" part, but it was too late now.

She'd flag him down, then take things from there.

Improvise. Be wild.

Head held high, Mel walked outside and stood on the sidewalk in front of her bungalow, waiting until the bright halogen beam of his motorcycle headlight approached down the street, then waved her arms frantically.

Let Project Seduce Adam Foster begin.

ADAM RODE home in the gathering twilight, deep in thought.

He'd been back in Point Beacon for a while now, and overall things were going well. Business was booming at Victory Vets Body Shop and Repair—the new business venture he'd started with his childhood best friend, James Bryant—and he'd even managed to reconnect with some of his old gang from high school.

Still, he felt a bit untethered.

Adam slowed at the four-way stop at Elm and Main before

proceeding through into the quiet suburbs surrounding their bustling tiny downtown. This place might be home, but returning here had been weird, especially since his dad had passed on. His mom had walked out when Adam was ten. This bike and the old run-down house at the end of Crestview Lane were his only inheritance, his only physical reminders of the life he'd had before the army. The mental reminders, on the other hand, were plentiful.

Tall trees blurred past. Everything looked the same as it had eight years ago when he'd left, but things were different, too. The townsfolk treated him like a hero now that he'd served his country. Before he'd enlisted, the good people of Point Beacon had labeled Adam a troublemaker—too wild, too reckless, too poor. They'd been right in most respects. Now, those same people thanked him for his service.

It was bizarre.

Veering around the corner onto his street, Adam caught sight of a woman flapping her arms like a chicken and did a double take. He slowed as he neared, and his heart skipped a beat.

Please, God, don't let it be Melody Bryant. Anybody but her.

But it was Mel. He'd recognize those frumpy clothes and great rack anywhere. Not that he ought to be checking her out, but he couldn't seem to help himself where she was concerned. All the more reason to steer clear. What he couldn't figure out, though, was why she was standing in the dark trying to take flight. James's little sister had always been a tad quirky, but he'd always kind of liked that about her. More than he should.

After taking a deep breath and steeling his natural inclination to fall back into their old patterns of easiness with her,

Adam slowed to a stop at the curb in front of where she stood. The home behind her reflected Mel to a T—prim, perfect, and polished to within an inch of its life. Basically, the exact opposite of him.

Once upon a time, he and Mel had been pretty good friends. He'd vanquished her bullies, and she'd nursed his wounds in the family's kitchen afterward when he'd stopped over to hang with James. She'd taped up his knuckles, then fed him M&Ms from her secret stash. The green ones had been her favorite. He still remembered that for some crazy reason.

He'd teased her about how they were supposed to make you horny...

Not helpful, bud.

Adam cut the bike's engine and watched her through the polarized glasses he wore to keep the bugs out of his eyes. Some people said a helmet would've been safer, but there was something about the wind through his hair and the slap of fresh air against his face that made him feel alive.

And it had been so long since Adam had felt truly alive, with a purpose and a reason to get out of bed in the morning besides work. Also, the law in this state didn't require him to wear one, so "those" people could go screw themselves.

Mel fidgeted under his steady gaze, the rose color staining her pretty cheeks softened by the glow from the porch light. Seemed he still affected her, even after all these years. The thought made him way happier than was wise.

He slid his glasses up to the top of his head and scratched his chin. Gritty and greasy from a long day working on cars, all Adam wanted was a cold beer and a long, hot shower. But if the determined look on Mel's face was any indication, he wouldn't be getting either for a while. "Can I help you with something?"

"Adam," she said, her voice a tad breathless. He felt that huskiness all the way to the tips of his booted toes but didn't let it show. This was little Melody Bryant, James's sister, a gal who was too good for him in high school and well out of his league now.

She was bossy, frustrating, opinionated.

Gorgeous.

Jag, one of the guys back at the shop, had told him she'd stopped by a week or so ago to schedule maintenance on her late-model Camry. Said the check engine light was on, but then she'd missed her appointment. Maybe that's why she wanted to talk to him tonight.

His gut said otherwise.

Adam shifted slightly in his seat, letting the burden of conversation fall on her. She was the one who'd flagged him down, after all, and he'd never been much good at small talk anyway. Then she bit her bottom lip, drawing his attention to how full and soft it looked and, despite his resolve, memories resurfaced of another night eight years prior—the two of them alone on the back porch of her parents' house, the feel of Mel's soft curves pressed against him as she'd whispered the words he'd never forget.

I love you, Adam Foster, and I want to give myself to you. Completely...

They'd both been so young, and he'd been totally blindsided.

"We need to talk." Mel cleared her throat, jarring him back to the present. Back then, he'd feared James would have him skinned alive if he'd known about that night, and everything since—their business partnership, their friendship, Adam's future—would've gone up in smoke. Now, he knew James had been keeping secrets of his own.

Mel stepped back from him a few feet and hiked her thumb toward the house. "Could you come inside for a minute, please?"

Adam exhaled slowly and carefully lowered the kickstand on his prized, fully customized Violet Pearl Softail Fat Boy before dismounting. It was the one decent thing his dad had left him, since the house was practically falling down. He pocketed his keys, then crossed his arms, assessing the woman in front of him.

Mel seemed shorter than he remembered, the top of her head barely reaching his chin as they stood there, staring at each other. Swallowing hard, he followed her up the short walk to her porch, the breeze carrying a hint of her cherry-blossom-and-vanilla scent. Lord help him, she practically had a neon sign above her head blinking Off-Limits, yet Adam's skin prickled with awareness. She was big trouble where he was concerned, and he'd be smart to keep as much distance between them as possible, literally and figuratively.

"Can we talk out here, if it's all the same?" he asked from the bottom of her stoop, while she stood near the door. He felt grungy and out of place with his oil-stained jeans and ripped black T-shirt and used that as an excuse. "I don't want to get your place dirty."

"Oh, uh..." Mel hesitated, her hand on the screen door.

Adam frowned. Was she trembling? Why was she trembling?

Beneath the recessed overhead lighting, her silky dark hair shimmered down her back, and an odd ripple of protectiveness surged through him. He'd promised to look after James's family until he returned next month from his last overseas deployment. Maybe that was the cause of the extra burst of testosterone rushing inside him, the nearly primal urge to stay close to Mel. That's what he was going with anyway. "Everything all right?"

When she didn't answer, his concern grew.

"If it's about the Camry, don't worry." He stepped up onto the bottom stair. "I'll tell the guys to work you into the schedule. I know you missed your appointment, so—"

"It's not about my car." Mel cut him off. "It's about..."

Growing up the hard way had taught Adam some valuable lessons. Mainly, if you had something difficult to do—like stealing from the local grocery store so your family wouldn't starve or chasing off the rich kids who were terrorizing your family's dog—then it was best to do it quick.

He raked a hand through his windblown hair and hung his glasses from the crew neck collar of his T-shirt. "Spit it out, Mel. I don't have all night."

She opened her eyes, pinning him to the spot with the same tenacious expression he'd seen on the face of many a solider in combat. Shoulders squared, she placed her hands on her hips and said the very last thing Adam ever expected to hear again.

"I need you to ruin my reputation."

CHAPTER TWO

Adam looked as flummoxed by her statement as Mel felt. Still, she couldn't regret saying it, though she probably should pull back a tad so she didn't scare him off before she'd even started. She gave a self-effacing chuckle, hoping to put him at ease. "Relax. It's not like I want you to do the ruining yourself."

Liar.

Heat rose in her cheeks as she waited for him to say something, anything. This was not going the way she'd envisioned things going in her mind. She'd pictured him being surprised, sure, but then he'd warm to the idea and agree, sweeping her into his arms and carrying her off to his rakish bedchamber to claim her body and soul and...

She'd obviously been reading too many historical romances again.

Okay. Fine. Given the way his tanned face had blanched,

she really shouldn't have blurted things out the way she had, but whenever Adam was around, her poised, precise persona seemed to go right out the window. One look from him and she was back to being the insecure, geeky kid who'd basically been his annoying shadow—always there, always silent.

Well, she was an adult now, and she refused to be silent anymore.

Despite his shock, she hoped the awkwardness between them would take care of itself eventually, along with other things.

If he agreed to help her.

"Just so I'm clear, what exactly is it you're asking me to do, Mel?" Adam's dark brows raised speculatively. He cleared his throat and smoothed his hands down the front of his jeans, clearly uncomfortable. She found it oddly endearing, seeing the cool bad boy of Point Beacon out of his depth.

Mel invited him into her kitchen for a drink. "I've got water or iced tea. There might be some soda in the garage. I can check. Oh, and there's half a bottle of merlot left from when Lilly came over the other night."

When he didn't respond, she turned back around to face him. And man, oh man, did he ever look breathtaking, slouched in the doorway, one broad shoulder leaning against the frame, his long legs crossed at the ankles. And Lord have mercy, those eyes of his—dark as midnight and twice as wicked.

Said eyes were currently narrowed on her, watching closely.

Summoning her last ounce of bravery, Mel continued. "I realize this probably comes as a strange request, considering we haven't seen each other in a while—"

"It's been eight years, Mel. This is the first time we've spoken since I came home."

True. He had her there, but it wasn't for lack of trying on her part.

She continued, thinking it best to just put it all out there before she couldn't anymore. The words rushed out in a nervous tumble. "I need a makeover. Everything from clothes to hair and makeup, but most especially, I need help with the social stuff. A coach who's in the dating trenches and knows their way around to show me what I'm doing wrong and teach me how to do things right. It has to be someone I can trust, someone who'll take this seriously and won't joke about it to other people behind my back. Someone who can keep a secret."

Oh, that had sounded good. She almost had herself convinced.

Adam shook his head and snorted, pushing away from the doorframe to step farther into the kitchen. The large room suddenly seemed smaller with his presence. "I don't know anything about all that makeover stuff, and I'm pretty sure my player reputation precedes me as far as dating is concerned. Can't Lilly help you with this?"

"No. She's got a worse dating reputation than you," Mel said, squeaking as the corner of the counter poked her in the butt. She hadn't realized she'd backed up until now.

The look Adam gave her sent a shot of awareness straight through Mel. The man could do more with one glance than most guys could do with a whole repertoire of foreplay. Or at least that's what she'd heard.

But she refused to be distracted here. She was in it to win it, darn it. She tamped down the persistent sizzle in her nervous system and lifted her chin. "Besides, she's trying to build her photography business and traveling a lot. I need someone close by who I can access for advice twenty-four-seven."

Adam stared at her for another long moment before looking away, a rueful smile curving his firm lips as he rocked back his heels. "You do know how hard it is to keep anything a secret in this town, right?"

"Yes." The word came out breathy because wow. When had it gotten so hot in there? Her chest squeezed and her pulse raced, and for a crazy second Mel wondered if she would pass out. And wouldn't *that* be just typical. If instead of luring Adam Foster, the man of her dreams, to her bed, she face-planted on the kitchen floor. The image of utter humiliation was enough to squelch her ardor for the time being, thank goodness. "And I need a guy's perspective."

I need you. It's always been you.

"Look, Mel, this isn't a good idea." His expression softened, and her knees tingled. "We have too much history, and James is my best friend, and if anything happened to you because of this harebrained scheme, I'd never forgive myself."

"Please," she implored, sensing her chance slipping away. "You're right. We do have history. We grew up together. You taught me how to play poker. We all used to hang out in my parents' basement. You know me better than anyone. That's how I know you can help me."

Tears stung the backs of her eyes, and Mel blinked hard to keep them at bay. She would not cry. She wouldn't. To distract herself, she toyed with the tiny pearl buttons on the front of her cardigan. "I know it might be a little awkward at first because of my whole crush on you back then, but I'm over all that, I promise. This is strictly business."

Adam sank down on one of the stools at her island, still not looking convinced. "This is a hell of a way to say howdy after all this time, Mel."

Was that a hint of humor she detected in his voice? She'd thought of all the men in the world, Adam would see her side of things. She'd thought he was different. Then again, she'd had him on a pedestal for so long, he was bound to fall off at some point.

Indignant anger stiffened her resolve, and she met his gaze direct. "This isn't a joke, Adam. I am not a joke. I thought I could trust you enough to ask for your assistance with my problem."

He turned away, mumbling what sounded like a curse under his breath. "Look, Mel. You've always had some cock-eyed vision of me as your knight in shining armor, but I'm not that guy. I never have been. The last time we talked about...*this*"—he gestured vaguely toward her then raked a hand through his hair, mussing it even more. "I said no. I thought that was the end of it."

Mel bit her lip as he stalked to the far side of the room, all lithe and graceful in those faded, stained jeans that perfectly cupping his tight butt. When Adam stopped and sighed, glancing back at her, she looked away fast, her cheeks hot. "Why me, Mel? The truth this time."

Guilt squeezed her chest, but she couldn't back down now. She'd come too far. "Because you're the coolest guy in town, the rebel. And if anyone can help me change my reputation, it's you."

Adam walked back to stand in front of her, his gaze traveling slowly over her from head to toe. She felt that look like a physical caress. "Why do you need a makeover? You look fine to me."

"*Fine?*" She gave a mirthless laugh and shook her head. "Fine has gotten me exactly nowhere. The guys around here don't want to date fine. And they certainly don't want to take fine to bed. I'm going to be twenty-five next month, and I'm still a virgin. How fine is that?"

His eyes widened, and Mel slapped her hand over her mouth. Yeah, she hadn't meant to say *that* much. Not tonight anyway.

Adam looked more curious now than interested.

Great. Mel crossed her arms. "Stop looking at me like a zoo exhibit. Some people stay virgins for a long time. Nothing wrong with it."

"But that's not what you want," Adam said.

"No, it's not." She gave a disgusted sigh. "I'm tired of being the best friend, the little sister, the sweet librarian who takes in stray cats and teaches kids to read on the weekends." Waldo meowed loudly and twined his way around her ankles. She closed her eyes. Okay, maybe she did like being those things, but she was also wanted to be so much more. "That's how everyone in this town sees me, if they notice me at all. I'm tired of being invisible. For once, I want a man to sit up and take notice. I want Point Beacon to see me for who I really am."

Mel swallowed hard, a sudden lump of sadness clogging her throat. She'd thought she was ready for this conversation with Adam, but obviously she wasn't. She didn't want to get emotional. In fact, she'd vowed not to, because the last thing she wanted to see in his eyes was pity.

He stared down at the floor, rubbing the back of his neck with one hand. "I'm sorry, Mel. I am." His deep, resigned tone echoed in the quiet kitchen. "But I'm not the right man for this job. You're an accomplished woman. You've got a college degree. You run that library like a well-oiled machine from what people tell me." He glanced up at her. "And you're selling yourself short. Any guy in town would be lucky to have you. If they can't see that, they don't deserve you."

She shifted her weight, wanting to scream. She was determined to lose her virginity before her birthday or die trying. With or without Adam's help. But man, oh man, did she want his help. She gave it one final shot. "Do me a favor. Stand up and take a step back."

Adam gave her a wary look but did so.

"Now look at me as a stranger." Mel smoothed a hand down her twinset and skirt and did her best to not fidget. "Tell me what you see."

Blood pounded loudly in her ears as she waited.

"I see a brilliant woman who gets things done, a hard worker. Someone dedicated, loyal, smart, caring, confident." He leaned his hip against the counter, as if expecting her to argue.

She did. "I might be confident at my job, but when it comes to dating, I'm lost. I refuse to spend the rest of my life alone and desperate."

Adam gave her a conciliatory smile, his teeth white and even against his tanned skin. "I'm sure the right guy will come along soon, Mel. Give it time."

"I've wasted enough time." She persisted. "Would you notice me in a crowd, Adam? I doubt it, since the first time you came over to my parents' house with James, you forgot I was even in the room."

"One time, Mel. That happened one time and you know it was because I was nervous. I told you that back then and it's still true now. Jeez. Can you please just drop this?"

They stared at each other until the tension in the room faded and they both ended up sitting on the stools again.

Mel shrugged a shoulder. "Lilly thinks I look like June Cleaver. The guy I went out with tonight couldn't get away from me soon enough. All the men I've dated around here aren't into me. There's only one factor present in all these equations. Me. I'm not cool. But you are. You can teach me, Adam. I know you can."

"Whatever." He scoffed and rubbed his chin again. "I'm sorry for what you're going through, Mel, but I just don't think—"

"I need to make changes." She wasn't above begging, feeling more desperate by the second as her chance with him slipped away. "You're right. Lilly can help me with some parts, but I still need a guy's perspective for the dating part, to point me in the right direction. You can't know what it's like, how lonely it is without any prospects for the future. I'm a mess."

Something flared in his dark eyes, there then gone so fast she couldn't identify it. Not anger. Understanding, maybe.

"You're not a mess," he said, taking her hand.

"Then you're either blind or a liar, Adam Foster." She pulled free, her skin tingling from his touch. "Lilly's right, I am June Cleaver. Or worse, I'm Marian the Librarian on steroids.

And I want more. More than being the predictable, boring, forgettable woman everyone in this town sets their clocks by." She wasn't letting him get away this time. "All I want is to learn how to sparkle."

"Mel," he said, his tone imploring. "You sparkle just fine on your own."

"There's that word again." She growled. "I swear if I hear one more 'fine' I'm going to—"

Adam held his hands up. "Maybe you're picking the wrong guys. Give it time. Nothing happens overnight."

The sympathy in his voice only set her off more. "Overnight? I'm going to be twenty-five in a month. Don't you think if the sparkle fairy was going to throw magic pixie dust my way, she would've done it by now?"

He straightened. "Based on the way you're laying into me right now, I don't think confidence is your problem at all."

She sighed. "There's something else. Something I haven't told anyone else yet. A regional position is opening up soon through the main library branch in Indy next month. It would be a huge promotion and the pay is higher. I'd still be in charge of the Point Beacon library, plus several others in the area. But in order to get it, I need to be able to schmooze the people making the hiring decision."

"Schmooze, huh?" Adam bent to pick up Waldo, and her pet purred so loud as he stroked its fur Mel got jealous. What she wouldn't give to change places with her cat right then. At last he said, "What happened, Mel? I don't get it. You always seemed so happy before I left."

Before I left. That was the crux of it. No one had ever held a candle to him in her heart. Maybe if she slept with him, she'd get him out of her system and finally be able to move on with her life. Not that she'd tell him that. She'd already told him too much already.

"Truth is, I don't want to play it safe anymore. Does that make sense? I want to go on dates and have fun and drink at the bar. I want to be the kind of woman people sit up and take notice of when they walk into a room. Basically, I want to be the female version of you, Adam. I want to fit into your world."

"Aw, Mel. You do fit." He put Waldo down and reached for her hand again, but she pulled away. If he touched her now, she'd start crying and all this would be over. "Everyone in town loves you. And appearances aren't everything."

She snorted. "No, but first impressions are."

He opened his mouth, then closed it again, exhaling.

Annoyance sparked anew inside her. "I've never once seen you take someone like me out to a club. Someone invisible."

Adam frowned. "Hey—"

"No." She stood and spun away fast. "All I want is a chance. One shot. We can even make a deadline, if it makes you feel better. August fourteenth, my birthday."

He tilted his head, his expression reluctant. "That doesn't give us much time."

"No, it doesn't." She grinned as she sensed victory. "Our end goal is Indy. You take me to one of the clubs you used to hang out in before you left for the Army on a practice date." Mel held out her hand. "Deal?"

"WAIT. YOU WANT ME TO 'PRACTICE' date you?" The earth as he knew it dropped out from beneath Adam's feet, but he managed to stay seated as he eyed her extended hand warily. "In Indy?"

"Here, too, if you think it would help," Mel said, when he didn't shake on her deal, instead using that hand to grab a large jar of M&M's sitting nearby, fishing out a handful. The gesture stirred all those old memories again. They'd once sat for an hour or more sorting them into piles of colors before arguing over who was going to get the green ones.

He shook off the memories of Mel's sweet laugh as she sat there twirling a piece of her silky hair around her finger. Like being this close to her again wasn't distraction enough, with her cherry scent tempting him to relax, to go ahead and agree with whatever craziness she spouted.

Mel was obviously going through something, and despite the fact that Adam still couldn't really understand the situation —clothes and makeup and men walking out on her after dinner —he definitely had no business thinking about how good she smelled.

Man, the guys he worked with at Victory Vets would be laughing themselves silly right now if they could see him. And James?

Well, James would kick his butt into next year if Adam did anything to hurt James's little sister, including acting on the totally inappropriate feelings Mel's request had stirred inside him.

So, no. Melody Bryant was strictly in the friend zone.

Besides, Adam didn't do relationships and Mel had forever written all over her. Guys like him didn't fall in love. Or if they did, it never worked out. He was too rough around the edges, had too much baggage from his past, wasn't a good prospect for long-term. He'd seen how unions fell apart and people destroyed one another when the very things that drew them together grew malignant and killed any love between them. No sense telling Mel all that, though, because they'd never get that far anyway.

Disappointment buzzed inside him like angry bees before he shook it off. It made no sense. He shouldn't be disappointed. He didn't want to get involved with Mel.

Do I?

She shook the canister at him again, jarring him out of his tangled thoughts. "Want some?"

It took Adam a minute to realize she was asking about the candy and not anything more. He took a handful of M&Ms and shoved them in his mouth, mainly so he didn't have to talk. He didn't trust his voice at the moment.

Undaunted, Mel continued as if her deal was a done thing. "I see my makeover as a two-parter. First we tackle my appearance, then we move to my social skills." She popped another green M&Ms in her mouth, and now Adam couldn't stop staring at her lips. "To give me confidence. In dating and in love."

"Whoa." Adam nearly choked on his chocolate. "How did we go from practice dating to finding love?"

Mel ignored his question. "I want a man not because I need one, but because I want a life partner. My ultimate goal is to find my person to share my life with." She narrowed her gaze on him, and heat prickled up his neck, making him long to run into the cool night and never look back, but his feet remained rooted to the spot. The air seemed to thicken and the area between his shoulder blades knotted and burned.

He knew that feeling. He'd felt it many times before. It was the one that said things were about to change, whether he was ready or not.

He hadn't been ready the day his mom had said she loved him, then walked out of his life forever. He hadn't been ready the day he'd gotten the call from the nurse on base saying his dad had died. He'd never been ready on the battlefield when they'd been ready to engage the enemy. And he sure as hell didn't feel ready now.

Mel was still talking, and Adam did his best to concentrate on what she was saying over the jackhammering of his own pulse in his ears. Then she stopped, her gaze concerned as she watched him. "Hey, you look like you're going to pass out on me. Don't worry. I'm not asking you to be *that* guy." She got up and filled a glass at the tap for him then shoved it into his numb fingers. "All I want if for you to teach how to date, how to attract a man and keep him past dinner."

Throat parched, he downed his water in one long gulp then plunked the empty glass down on the granite-topped island. *Move.* He needed to move, to pace, to get some space to process what she'd told him.

In the military, he'd used the long, grueling morning work-outs for that purpose. They kept him strong and focused and clear.

If only he could take a twenty-mile hike now to get his head back on straight. As it was, he was trapped here, in her tiny kitchen, with her candy smiles and sweet cherry scent. "I don't know, Mel. I don't think I'm the person you think I am. Until recently, Point Beacon didn't think very highly of me. You said it yourself. I'm the resident bad boy. People will definitely talk if you start hanging out with me. You don't want to deal with that. Trust me."

Mel sat back down, her shoulders slumping. His first instinct was to make it all better. Which made no sense because most days he barely had his own life under control, what with the garage still in its fledgling year and him trying to establish some new kind of normal after the Army. His life was kind of a mess. He had no business considering trying to help anyone else improve theirs.

"It might be a nice change, actually," Mel said, her voice a bit unsteady. "Right now, all they talk about is how I'm so predictable that they can set watches by me."

In the end, it was the catch in her breath that did him in. Tears got him every time. They'd worked on him the night on the porch eight years ago when Mel had kissed him, the memory seared into his soul for eternity. Back then, he'd found the strength to walk away.

Tonight, he prayed he could do it again.

Because it was the right thing to do. Because it was the best thing for Mel, even if she didn't see it.

Because it was the best thing for him, too.

Isn't it?

He took a deep breath, fortifying his defenses. "Look, I'm flattered and all, but this makes no sense."

Her sad little sigh dug sharp claws into his scarred heart. "You know me, Adam. You've seen me at my worst, and you've never judged me. I know your reputation, but I also know that when you think no one's looking you're gentle and patient and kind. Most importantly, I know you'd never hurt me. That's why I chose you."

Wow. He sat there, speechless. He didn't deserve her praise, no matter how much he craved it.

Then Mel snorted. "Plus, you're scorching hot, which doesn't hurt either." She grinned in the face of his shock. "Oops. Did I say that out loud? Sorry."

Adam chuckled uncomfortably. The fact she found him attractive made his ego and certain body parts take notice, but his rational brain warned it was a terrible mistake. Turmoil churned inside him as Mel got him more water, plus a glass for herself.

There was one other huge gorilla of a problem he hadn't brought up before, but that could have a huge impact on his life if he got involved in this ill-advised project of hers.

"What about the garage?" Adam asked at last.

"What about it?" Mel frowned.

"Victory Vets is all I have right now. It's my main source of income and my future, if it goes well. It takes up most of my time and I'm partners in the venture with your brother. If this makeover goes south for some reason, that could have huge impacts on my life." He arranged a tiny pile of red M&Ms on the island into a frowning face with his finger. "Not to mention that your parents will flip out if we go on a date together, even a practice one. And they'll have questions about why we're spending so much time together all the sudden. What will you tell them? Are you prepared to lie to them about what's going on?"

She didn't seem to have an answer for that ready, and he seized on what was probably his last opportunity to get the hell out of this mess. "Look, Mel. I'd like to help, but your brother is my best friend and business partner. And your family is the only one I have left. I can't risk all that, and if you really care about me, you shouldn't ask me to."

Mel gave a slow nod, staring down at her own candy on the counter, arranged into a blue smiley face. She'd always looked on the bright side, always been optimistic. Loyal too. She'd never wavered from his side during high school, no matter how many stupid mistakes he'd made, no matter how bad his reputation had gotten, no matter how many times he'd tried to push her and everyone else who'd cared for him away because love only ever brought pain and heartache.

All of it made turning down her request so much harder, no matter what was at stake for him.

"We wouldn't have to lie to people. We could just redirect their attention elsewhere," Mel said, eventually. "And just so you know, I don't see my parents every day anymore. I even miss Sunday dinners sometimes now with James gone."

That surprised him. Back in the day, the Bryant family Sunday dinners had been sacred. The whole family was there, including Adam. No one missed unless you were dead. Or deployed.

Huh. Perhaps his Mel had changed after all.

My Mel?

His chest squeezed. No. She wasn't his Mel. Never would be.

But it was a nice dream.

"And I promise that if things don't work out, I'll take full responsibility with James, my parents, the whole town. It will be my fault, not yours. You won't lose anything." When he still didn't respond, she added, "C'mon. It'll be fun. You can play Professor Higgins to my Eliza Doolittle."

He gave her a funny look. He'd never heard of either of those people.

"You know. *My Fair Lady?*" Mel gave him an inquiring stare. "'The Rain in Spain'?"

When he still didn't get it, she shook her head, resting her hand on his forearm. Awareness blazed through Adam's blood like lit gasoline, and he covered her hand with his without thinking. He hated the idea of going behind her parents' back. They'd been there for him when he'd had no place else to go. They'd become like his second mother and father. They'd supported him through all his major milestones—birthdays, graduations, even basic training.

Everything.

Then Adam stroked Mel's soft skin with his thumb, and for the first time he saw her, truly saw her—with her old-lady sweater set and her below-the-calf skirt, hiding what he suspected was a great pair of legs. Maybe it wouldn't hurt to help her find her freedom, rediscover her joy, restore her faith in herself, and make her see the beauty he saw in her.

But he also didn't miss the glint of adoration in her green eyes when she looked at him. Mel had him pegged wrong.

She thought his life was so great, but that wasn't reality. He wasn't brave or confident or popular. And though he owed her more than he could ever repay, the dating part could never happen, fake or otherwise. Even though he'd learned way more about Mel in the last hour than he'd ever known in the years prior. Even though he respected her more than any other woman alive. Even though he liked her so much it hurt...he couldn't.

Because, if he was honest, he wanted the same thing she did: love. Someone to share his future with, someone special in his life. Remote as that possibility seemed, given the closest thing he'd ever found in those clubs in Indy she wanted to go to were meaningless one-night stands.

Truth was, Adam had no idea how to find a life partner—not for Mel and certainly not for himself. Her project was basically a big red warning stripe, complete with neon and flashing lights telling him to run, far and fast.

But he couldn't say all that to her, so he sat there instead, covering Mel's hand on his arm with his, studying her from beneath his lashes while she stared at her shoes. He hated hearing her put herself down. The way she'd described the situation, she felt like the most boring person on earth. And yeah, she wasn't the typical popular, party gal, but that didn't mean she wasn't perfect in her own way.

Uncomfortable stabs of protectiveness forced him to his feet, making him let her go before he couldn't anymore. His apology rushed out, mirroring all the chaos he felt inside. "I'm sorry."

Mel looked up at him then, frowning, the sadness in her gaze nearly driving him to his knees. "Me too. I guess I'll stay alone and die with a dozen cats."

"Come on, Mel," he pleaded. "Be serious."

"I *am* serious. I have no game. No magical unicorn powers to bring all the boys to my yard. I need help. I need the tools. And I need experience. And please don't give me that crap about saving myself for someone special. I dare you to sit there and tell me that every time you've been with a woman, it was more than just sex."

Well, she had him there. He'd never been embarrassed discussing sex before, but suddenly his skin felt too tight for his body, and perspiration dotted his forehead. He'd kept that information out of his mind because thinking about the fact that Mel was still innocent, still a virgin, made his palms itch.

All he could think about now was that long-ago night, the shadows soft and the crickets chirping low, when she'd whispered in his ear, *"I love you, Adam Foster, and I want to give myself to you. Completely..."*

He forced words past his constricted vocal cords. "I've made mistakes. You don't have to."

"Men don't want inexperienced women." She glared. "Who wants to go to bed with a fumbling idiot? I want to know what I'm doing. I want to drive my partner crazy with lust. I want all the closeness and touching and searing looks in public. I want it all."

Adam's breath seized. He wanted that, too, so much he ached. But he knew that didn't last. Which made this whole situation even more off-limits.

His own parents hadn't been able to keep their hands off each other at first and look how that had turned out. Watching them annihilate their relationship had put him off love for good.

But being home, being alone, made him feel lonely more and more often. Or he was getting mushy in his old age. He was only twenty-seven, but some days he felt like a hundred.

Especially since many of his friends were getting married now, like Miguel at the garage. He certainly believed the whole happily-ever-after thing *was* possible, even if Adam though it was just a pretty fairy tale.

"Adam?" Mel's voice brought him back to the present.

He stood on not-quite-steady legs, feeling bewildered and bothered and totally discombobulated. He wanted to help her, he did. But honestly, he couldn't even help himself right now.

"I'm beyond flattered you asked me, really," he said, backing toward the hall and the exit beyond. "But I'm not the man for this job, Mel."

CHAPTER THREE

el walked into the living room as the front door closed behind Adam. Her sadness only worsened as the sound of his bike engine faded away into the night. Waldo purred, following her. She picked him up, then settled on the sofa, feeling...empty.

She'd never really considered him saying no. Now she needed moral support to bolster her flagging spirits. She grabbed her phone from the coffee table where she'd dropped it earlier and dialed Lily's number.

Her best friend answered on the first ring, and Mel poured out her story of the past hour, nuzzling Waldo's furry head in-between tears.

"Oh, hon. I'm so sorry. Are you okay?" Lilly asked when she was done. "Want me to go to Victory Vets tomorrow and kick his butt for you?"

"No." Mel swiped her hand across her damp cheeks. "I guess I just expected... *more*."

"Well, that was your first mistake." Lilly sighed. "Never count on a guy for 'more.' I've learned that the hard way."

Mel winced at the edge in her best friend's voice. The sharpness rivaled any scalpel. Waldo jumped down, and Mel sat up, doing her best to shake off the melancholy that had set in after unloading all her angst over Adam's rejection. "I'm not sure what to do now. He was basically my whole idea."

"Mistake two, hon. Never bet on only one stallion." Lilly sighed. "What you need now is a plan B. You've already done the hardest part—deciding to make a change. Don't let this bump in the road stop you."

Only problem was, Mel's feelings for Adam seemed more like a Mount Everest-size issue than a tiny molehill.

Besides, she was so tired of the dating treadmill. And the thought of more failed first dates, more online searches, more mixing and mingling...

Ugh. It all sounded tedious, daunting, and depressing.

"Mel? You still there?" Lilly asked. "C'mon, girl. Don't give up."

"I don't know." Mel flopped back against the cushions and looked up at the ceiling as she thought about the M&Ms in the kitchen. How they'd both arranged them on the counter. Adam had never once made fun of her little obsession for orderliness. He'd just gone along with it, as if it was the most normal thing in the world. Like she was normal.

Fresh tears prickled behind her eyes and Mel angrily blinked them away. This was ridiculous. She was tired of crying. She'd been rejected plenty of times in the last few months and she'd always gotten oner it. Lilly was right. She wasn't a quitter. She needed to get back out there and get the job done.

Resolved, Mel pushed to her feet and back into the kitchen to shove the candy jar back into its spot in the corner, the phone tucked between her jaw and shoulder. "Fine. I'll go ahead with the makeover on my own. Then I'll worry about dating."

"I'll help, too. When's your next day off?"

"This Friday. Why?"

"Let me see if I can get you an appointment with my stylist at the salon I use in Indy. I'll try to take the day off, too, to go with you. Marguerite's great. We'll get your hair and makeup done, the works. Then we can do lunch and shopping before we come home." Lilly's smile was evident through her voice. "I bet once the men of Point Beacon get a load of the new Melody Bryant, your perpetual virginity problem will take care of itself."

Mel snorted as she slid Adam's dirty glass into the dishwasher. A glance at the clock above the stove showed it was close to ten now. She had to be up early for work in the morning. Tuesday was senior day, and they bused patrons in from all the surrounding towns for lectures and crafts and all sorts of literary fun. "Let's hope so. Okay, I need to go. Thanks for listening, and we'll talk again tomorrow."

After she ended the call, Mel stared at her reflection in the dark window over the sink. Her conservative outfit seemed too snug and out of place now. Not that she wanted to run around in lingerie, but things needed to change. She needed to change. No more dressing for comfort in outdated clothes.

No more hiding.

She knew the upscale salon Lilly went to was located in a

trendy suburban mall on Indy's northwest side called Copper-field Downs. Mel had been there once and had marveled at all the designer boutiques. No more shopping the clearance rack at the local secondhand store because the thought of going into a fashionable store in the big city was too intimidating.

For the first time since Adam had kindly kicked her to the curb, Mel's anticipation grew.

After locking up her house and turning off the lights for the night, she practically skipped to bed with Waldo in tow.

Change was definitely in the air.

ADAM TOOK a slow ride around town once he left Mel's house, hoping to calm his racing mind. Point Beacon wasn't big, just under six thousand residents, so the grand tour didn't take long. In the end, he wound up back at Victory Vets because it was his go-to place in town for peace. When the world outside got too nuts, when memories of his time in the military haunted his dreams, when the gnawing loneliness of being alone in the world threatened to take him under, this was where he came. There was something about tinkering with greasy old engine parts that soothed his savage beast.

Now, though, even as he was hard at work tearing apart a Hemi V8 to locate the source of leaking fluid, he couldn't seem to get Mel and the things she'd told him earlier out of his head. She'd been so open, so vulnerable.

So available.

Nope. No, no, no.

He'd made the right choice, walking away. She'd needed

help, but she was far better off without him. He'd only cause her trouble, because that's what he did. Lord knew his dad had beat that into him enough as a kid. He wasn't good enough, wasn't smart enough, wasn't successful enough for a woman like Mel.

Chicken.

And yeah, she scared him too. Not because he couldn't see himself with her but because he could. He'd told her the truth, though, he couldn't risk all the good things he had now. They were all he had left.

A key grated in the door lock, and Adam peered around the side of the hood of the pickup to see who was there at this ungodly hour.

Miguel, his second-in-command, strolled into the garage. "What's up, dude? I saw the lights on and thought somebody was breaking in. It's after midnight. What are you doing here?"

"I could ask you the same thing." Adam wiped his greasy hands on a towel. They'd served together in Syria and survived some of the worst firefights side by side. Experiences like that forged bonds stronger than steel. His old friend looked tired tonight, though, evidenced by the dark circles under Miguel's eyes. Probably because he and his fiancée were expecting a baby on top of planning a wedding. He doubted poor Miguel was getting much sleep these days.

"Everything okay at home?" Adam asked him.

"Yep." Miguel flashed a tired smile. "Camille's craving ice cream and bacon, so I was sent to the store to get some. What about you? Lady troubles again?"

Adam shrugged, then went back to working on the truck engine. He didn't really want to get into what happened with him and Mel tonight, especially with Miguel. The guy was far too perceptive for his own good. That's what had made them both such great soldiers and what made them such pains in the ass as friends sometimes. With Miguel you got all honesty, all the time.

"Uh-huh." Miguel leaned in beneath the other side of the truck's open hood. "I see."

"What?" Adam growled, not looking up.

"Go ahead and tell me about her."

"There is no 'her.'" Adam straightened so quickly he nearly conked his head on the hood. "I'm not interested in dating anybody. You know that."

Miguel fiddled with the fuel lines. "Don't have to date someone to have problems. Look at Jag and Hollywood."

Michael "Jag" Collins had recently joined their staff at Victory Vets. He was an excellent mechanic, despite losing an arm courtesy of a bombing in Yemen. He'd been with the navy's legal corps, thus the nickname. And Hollywood was actually Sara Deacons. She'd been in the coast guard out in California and had been the best marine mechanic on the West Coast. Her nickname came from her talent with explosives, grand enough to rival any John Wick movie.

Adam had always thought maybe there was an attraction between Hollywood and fast-talking, hard-living Jag, but it was only a hunch. Anyway, Sara had gotten herself caught up in some nonsense on base one night and asked for an early discharge. She didn't talk about it, and the guys at Victory Vets didn't ask. It was an unwritten rule. Still, she and Jag were always betting each other to do dumb stuff, always trying to show each other up. It was a bit too competitive for Adam's tastes, but whatever floated their boats, he supposed.

Miguel was still staring at Adam, one brow raised, waiting for a response. The guy could wait all night for all Adam cared.

He got back to work under the hood, as much to avoid answering his friend as to straighten out his own thoughts.

Mel wasn't so much a problem as she was a temptation. One he'd be wise to steer clear of. His head knew that. Now if someone would just tell the rest of him, he'd be all set.

She was untouchable. She was off-limits.

She was so darned cute.

The screwdriver slipped, cutting Adam's thumb. "Son of a—"

He yanked his hand out of the truck and walked over the nearby sink to wash his hands. Mel was turning into a distraction he didn't need.

One night, one conversation, one reunion was all it took to get her stuck in his craw again, not that she'd ever really gone far. She'd been a part of his life since he'd met James in high school.

She felt like family, but she wasn't. Not really.

The whole time Adam bandaged his cut, he felt the weight of Miguel's gaze on him, watching him, silently mocking him, most likely. God, was he that obvious?

"You might as well tell me who she is," Miguel said, walking over to where Adam stood near the first aid kit. "I'll find out anyway, eventually."

"Huh?" Adam said, trying to play dumb.

It didn't work. Miguel persisted. "Hey, I understand. The first time I met Camille, she knocked me for such a loop, I didn't know whether I was coming or going for weeks. Got all those warm fuzzies and crap. It was awful."

Adam shook his head, chuckling. He was acting like an idiot and he knew it, but man. Little Melody Bryant, all grown up and asking him to practice date her and teach her all about men and sex? How the hell was he supposed to cope with that?

"Sorry." Adam winced as he closed the first aid kit and returned to the truck. "You're right. I got *a thing* going on."

"Say that again."

"A thing?"

"No. The me being right part. I never hear that anymore, so I want to savor it." Miguel snorted. "And what kind of 'thing' exactly?" He waggled his brows. "You hook up with another garage groupie? The blonde? Jag said he was gonna try to tap that, too."

"Jag's an idiot." Adam sighed. "And no. This is someone I knew before I got deployed. I'm not tapping anything."

"Ah, an old flame."

"No. More like an old friend." Mel had been his friend, a good one. At least, before she'd offered herself up to him that night on her parents' porch and things between them had gotten weird. He'd figured that was all in the past though, until she'd basically done the same thing again tonight. He liked directness, in life and in Mel.

More than he should.

Adam exhaled and got back to tinkering with the engine. He shouldn't go there. He *hadn't* gone there with Mel, even though she'd all but begged him to. Twice. They should give him a medal for his frigging fortitude.

But each time he thought of Mel—her big green eyes so full

of hope and hurt, her silky dark hair rippling down her back in soft waves. Hell, even her prim library clothes that hugged her curves in all the right places—it combined to make Adam question the wisdom of his choices.

The trouble was though that he knew better than to think Mel would give up on this crazy scheme of hers just because he'd turned her down. Once she got an idea in her head, she followed through. So, if he was crossed off her list, she'd move on to the next option. A man who might not be as chivalrous as Adam. And the thought of some dude pawing and pushing Mel to do things she wasn't ready for made his blood burn.

Gah! He hadn't thought about that before, but he should have. If anyone was going to teach Mel how to attract a guy, it should be him.

Except, it shouldn't.

Right?

Adam pried off a stubborn oil cap with more force than necessary. He was in a horrible Catch 22 here, right back where he'd started again. Work wasn't even helping at all tonight.

Frustrated, he straightened and tossed his tools aside. He was tired and stressed and in no mood or frame of mind to even consider this mess right now. Time to go home and go to bed.

Miguel waited for him by the exit while Adam shut off the lights. They walked out into the warm early July night together.

"So, what are you gonna do about this woman?" Miguel asked.

"No idea, man," Adam said as he swung his leg over his bike and started the engine. "Now get that bacon and get home to your fiancée, dude. And don't forget the ice cream."

CHAPTER FOUR

"I thought we were waiting until Friday to start the makeover," Mel said as Lilly slid a plaid headband out of Mel's hair. "That's still two days away."

"Oh, I already made you an appointment to see my stylist," Lilly said. "Consider this a little experiment first. Now lean forward and shake your head."

Mel did so, then rose to see her reflection in the bathroom mirror. Great. Now she wasn't just dowdy, she looked like Cousin Itt. She blew the hair from her face, giving Lilly a dubious glance. "This isn't going to work."

All her doubt demons crawled out of their hiding spots. Even here, in the privacy of her own home, she already felt naked without her trusty headband. And if she felt that way *here*, what in the world would happen when she set foot in a bar?

"Yes, it is." Lilly turned her around and forced Mel to sit on the edge of the tub. "We're not doing anything drastic tonight, just trying out a new hairstyle and some makeup. That dress of mine looks super cute on you, too." As Lilly talked, she smoothed a comb through Mel's hair, slicking it back into a sleek ponytail at the nape of her neck. She clipped in a chunky barrette to hold it in place, then spritzed Mel with some flowery-smelling hairspray. "There. Nice and sophisticated. And your widow's peak is a unique touch."

"Right. Maybe if my name's Morticia Addams." Mel stood and stared at her reflection in the mirror above the vanity, tugging at the skirt of the bright crimson minidress that felt way too short for her comfort.

"Whatever." Lilly rolled her eyes. "It's already way better than your usual style. Now let me put some makeup on you, and you'll be all set."

"I don't know, Lils." Mel scrunched her nose. "I'm too tired to go out. Maybe I should just go to bed."

"You can sleep later." Her best friend positioned Mel under the vanity lights, then opened the elaborate makeup case she'd brought along. There were all sorts of pots and little jars containing every glittery color of the rainbow. "It would be a shame to get you glammed up just to wash it all off afterward. Besides, I already told Dom we'd meet him and his friends at the Black Dog."

"What?" Mel tried to move away, but Lilly blocked her. Dominic D'Angelo owned the local tire store and had been dating Lilly for nearly a month. That had to be some kind of record where her bestie was concerned. "Now I'll be the third wheel, too? No thanks. Besides, I have to work tomorrow."

"It's Wednesday. Everyone has to work tomorrow."

Lilly set about smearing cream on Mel's face. Next came

powder and blush and eye shadow and liner and a shade of lipstick that looked like a cross between Rudolph's nose and a stop sign. "C'mon. It'll just be for an hour. We walk in, say hello, have a drink, then come home. Simple."

Simple for her, maybe. Lilly was funny and easy to talk to. Men liked her.

"Adam Foster might be there," Lilly added as she applied a final coat of mascara to Mel's lashes. "Dom's good friends with the guys at Victory Vets and hangs out with them a lot."

"Then I'm definitely not going." Mel darted left this time when Lilly went right and gained her freedom. On her way out the door, though, Mel locked eyes with a stranger in the mirror and stopped short. It was her, but a version she'd never seen before. This Mel looked sassy and bright and, well... *sparkly.*

"What do you think?" Lils peered over Mel's shoulder. "Pretty good, eh?"

It didn't suck. Mel smacked her lips together, tasting the cherry gloss slicked on top of the lipstick to give it a little shimmer. Having her hair pulled back from her face revealed her bone structure—high cheekbones and a pointed chin. The widow's peak still bothered her, but overall, even Mel had to admit she was impressed. Lilly did the makeup for some of her photography clients, too, and Mel could see now why her best friend held the title of "Point Beacon's Most Flattering Portraitist."

"Thank you," she said finally, unable to look away from her own reflection.

"You're welcome." Lils applied some of the same gloss to her own lips before leading Mel out of the bathroom. "Now get your shoes and bag or we'll be late."

"I don't know—"

"I do." Lilly pointed at the pair of red flats she'd lent Mel to match the slinky rayon halter-style minidress, then grabbed both their purses. "We are *so* doing this. Ready?"

In the end, the possibility of showing Adam what he was missing was too good an opportunity to pass up. She could do this.

She would do this.

Shoulders squared, Mel walked to the front door. "Ready."

"Good." Lilly grinned. "Don't overthink this. You look fabulous."

Fifteen minutes later, they were in the Black Dog Pub, a typical small-town bar with lots of rowdy patrons and local memorabilia on the walls. The smells of fried food and beer filled the air, along with cheers and jeers from a group of customers in the corner rooting for their favorite baseball team on the flat-screen TV mounted from the ceiling.

At first, the same old fears threatened to sabotage Mel's newfound courage, but she forced herself to stay strong. A few people caught her eye as she and Lilly made their way across the crowded, dimly lit room. Two guys in suits and loosened ties gave Mel lopsided smiles, looking her up and down. That was a good sign, right? Frankly, it was more interest than she'd ever gotten from one of her dates. Heck, the second guy even winked at her.

Feeling a confidence boost, Mel grinned back. That earned her a leering catcall.

She frowned. Okay, maybe not so good after all. She wanted to be the life of the party as much as the next gal, but she also didn't want to be treated like a side of choice beef. She tugged her tiny dress down farther to make sure everything was still covered, just in case.

At last, they reached the far corner of the room and the rowdy table, which turned out to be Dom and the guys from Victory Vets.

"Hey, baby." Lilly dropped a quick kiss on Dom's cheek. "You all know Mel, yes?"

Lilly tugged her forward.

Mel saw Adam sitting at the end of the table, along with other mechanics from his garage. Lordy, the guy could fill out a black T-shirt like nobody's business, all lean sinew and hard muscle. His hair was tamed tonight, combed back to reveal his gorgeous dark eyes. There was a tightness to his jaw though as he took her in, and Mel felt the insane urge to run her tongue over that rigid line, then down his neck, to see if he tasted as good as he looked.

"Hey, ladies." Dom grabbed a couple of spare chairs for them. "Have a seat."

"Thanks." Mel squeezed in between Adam and Jag.

"You, uh, look different tonight," Adam said, watching her.

Not exactly the compliment she'd been hoping for, but having his undivided attention made her insides quiver. Still, she wanted to show him he wasn't the only fish in the pond, so she turned to Jag instead. Except he was focused solely on the game on TV, which was going into its ninth inning, from what the announcer said.

"How are things at the garage, Jag?" Mel asked him loudly, hoping to gain the guy's attention. Not exactly world-class small talk, but it would have to do on such short notice.

Jag grunted in answer, fumbling for his beer on the table without taking his eyes off the screen.

Meanwhile, those two guys in suits at the bar that had catcalled her earlier were moving closer, still spewing lewd remarks in her direction. Mel's stomach clenched, and she gave a nervous glance in Adam's direction to see if he'd heard.

Yeah, based on his darkening scowl and the glare he shot the two suits, he'd heard. Then next thing she knew, Adam had stood and taken her by the arm. "Can I speak to you for a minute, Mel?"

He led her to a secluded hallway near the restrooms, sticking closer to her side the whole way as if wanting to block her from any prying views. Once they were alone, he asked, "What the hell are you doing?"

Hurt and anger welled up inside her at his icy tone. He'd had his chance to help her the other night, and he'd turned her down. He had no right to an opinion anymore. She could wear what she liked, do what she liked, with anyone she liked. Mel lifted her chin defiantly. "Lilly came over and asked me to go out. Why do you care?"

"Because I promise James I'd look out for his family until he got back." His voice, deep and hard, sent a chill down her spine. Adam turned to shoot a scathing look at the two suited idiot who'd returned to the bar the second they'd seen Adam. Then he turned back to Mel and took her chin between his fingers as he gave her a head-to-toe appraisal. "Did Lilly do this?"

"Yes." Mel shook off his touch, ignoring the thrum of her pulse and sizzle of nerve endings from his closeness. Adam under normal circumstances as a brooding bad boy was dangerous enough to her heart. Adam when he got all alpha-protective? Well, that was downright lethal. She battled the tingle in her traitorous knees and said, "Why? Are you jealous?"

"I'm not jealous. I'm concerned." He rested his palm on the wall beside her head, his heat surrounding her as his expression softened into something far worse than anger. Pity.

Her eyes stung, and she bit her lip hard. She would not cry. Not here. That would only make this night even worse. Despite her efforts, Adam's gorgeous face blurred as hot tears welled over and slid down her cheeks. She should have stayed home. She really was as pathetic as everyone in this town thought she was.

***

ADAM SWORE SOFTLY and hung his head. He hadn't meant to make her cry. He'd only wanted to show her the kinds of threats those jackal playboys who frequented this place could pose to her. He should know. Hell, he'd been one of them on occasion. Not that he was proud of it.

Adam grabbed a napkin off the nearby service cart for her as he wrestled with his own guilt. Because he'd not been completely honest. He wasn't jealous necessarily, but he also wasn't okay with other men ogling Mel's assets, either, especially when they didn't appreciate all her other wonderful qualities, like her intelligence and her humor and her kindness. It didn't matter what she was wearing. It was a free country. She had the right to wear what she wanted without being harassed for it. Still, the thought of those two punks drooling over Mel's gorgeous curves made him want to slam a fist into their faces to prove his point.

He turned back to face Mel again, once more stunned by how she looked tonight. Every time he'd seen her since he'd been back in town, she'd always looked professional, prim, and proper. Now, she looked vibrant and free and, well...scorching hot. Which made it all the harder to keep her where she needed to be in his mind.

A tidy friend-zone box, with a side of best friend's little sis.

Thinking of Mel that way helped Adam stay on the straight and narrow where she was concerned. But in that little red dress, with legs up to there and a neckline cut low enough to offer a tantalizing hint of the soft curves beneath, adrenaline shot straight southward for Adam. Oh boy. He was in trouble here.

Then Mel sniffled, and empathy joined the confusing rush of emotions flooding his system. Adam sighed. "Please don't cry."

"Why not? This evening has become a disaster already." She fiddled with her napkin and her hands brushed his chest, sending tingles of need through his torso.

He stepped back and raked a hand through his hair, searching for his lost control. "It's not that bad, Mel. Just not your usual crowd."

"Great. That's exactly what I was going for. Not." She threw up her hands in exasperation. "Now you see why I need your help? I can't believe you turned me down. After I laid out all my faults in excruciating detail to you the other night too." More tears welled as she sagged back against the wall. Adam took a step closer, glancing around to make sure no one was watching them. Her sweet scent surrounded him once more—sweet cherry blossoms and vanilla, mixed tonight with a hint of roses from whatever stuff she'd used in her hair. It chased away the harsh environment of the pub, and he forced himself to focus on the graffiti-carved wooden wall behind her head and not how the warmth of her penetrated the front of his T-shirt, beckoning him closer. Because if he thought about that, Adam wasn't sure he could stop himself from gathering her into his arms and resting his cheek atop her silky hair to comfort her. "Don't be upset."

"I'm not crying because I'm upset, Adam. I'm crying because I'm frustrated." Her words were muffled by the napkin, and he had to strain to hear them over the din in the bar and the race of blood in his ears.

Adam did his best to distract himself by recalling the past. "Remember when you were a kid and you and James would fight? Your face would get all red and scrunched up and you'd scream at him and sob all at the same time. Like that little angry dude in the animated emotions movie, with the flames shooting out the top of his head."

She smacked him on the arm, but she also laughed, a good sign in Adam's book.

He put a little distance between them again as Mel dabbed away the tears from her cheeks. "Can you grab my purse from the table? I want to check my makeup."

"Sure thing." He got it, then returned to her side in seconds. The last thing he wanted was for one of those idiots in the suits to come over and try to pick her up right now. She was too vulnerable. Mel needed someone to look out for her.

She offered you that job.

His gut knotted. Yeah, she had. And he'd turned it down.

"Oh, no." Mel tried to wipe away the smudges of mascara staining the skin beneath her eyes with one hand while holding a tiny mirror with the other, but all it ended up doing was make her look like a raccoon. "This is worse than the time I got painted like the Joker at the state fair."

Her eyes met Adam's over the top of her mirror, and they stared at each other for along second before cracking up completely, the unbearable tension that had started inside him the minute he'd seen her walk up to the table tonight dissipating until Adam could finally breathe again.

Mel's laughter drifted over him like the wind chimes his mom had hung from the front of their house when he'd been a toddler. They'd fascinated him with their lilting, soothing quality. He felt the same way now—enchanted, mesmerized.

Whoa there, cowboy.

He couldn't fall down that slippery slope of attraction to Mel again, because each time he did, it got more difficult to find his way back up to reality. And the reality was that helping Mel with her "special project" would be nothing short of stupid. Bad enough he'd dreamed about her last night. About her crooked little grin and how he wished he could make her smile like that forever.

He'd never survive if they spent 24-7 together working to get her a decent date.

"Oh well." Mel straightened at last, pushing away from the wall to smooth a hand down the front of her tiny dress. "Back to the trenches."

"Wait." Adam placed his other hand on the wall beside her, caging her in before he realized what he was doing. All he knew was he didn't want her to go. Not yet. "You don't have to do this, Mel. The whole makeover thing."

"Yeah, I do." She blinked up at him with those pretty green eyes, so bright and innocent and determined. "I need to do this. For me."

His head was a mess, his instincts torn and twisted. He'd known Mel for years. He'd seen her strength, her resilience. He knew she wouldn't give up until she achieved her goal, one way or the other. And yes, he had a lot on the line here, but he couldn't just sit by on the sidelines and watch her put herself out there like that without knowing what would happen. Which meant Adam had to make a choice. Actively participate, where at least he could work to keep Mel safe and protected, or make sure he didn't see her again until it was all over. Which in a town the size of Point Beacon would be close to impossible. So, in the end, there was no choice at all.

"What other plans does Lilly have for you?" he asked.

Mel shrugged. "She got me an appointment with her salon in Indy this Friday. Then we were going to have lunch and shop afterward for a new wardrobe."

"I'll come too," Adam said before he thought better of it. "I'll take the day off from the garage. If you still want me to help you, that is."

She blinked at him, looking about as shocked as he felt. "Yes, I still want you to help me."

"Good. Now, the ground rules." He'd dug himself into a hole here, but he wanted to make sure they could both escape as unscathed as possible at the end. The rest he'd figure out along the way. "I'll help with the makeover and pointers about men and dating, but that's it. No practice dates. And no sex. Not between us anyway. Deal?"

He extended a hand to her as she'd done to him the other night.

Mel hesitated, then shook on it. "Okay. Deal."

Adam wanted to run, wanted to hide, but he'd made a promise, and he didn't break them. And sure, Mel seemed to affect him more than any other woman had in a long time. It was because he'd been alone too long that was all.

She was way too good for him. Way out of his league.

The knowing didn't stop the wanting.

When he realized they were both just standing there, staring at each other, he cleared his throat and gestured for Mel to proceed him out of the hallway. "Great. Let's get started then."

CHAPTER FIVE

Friday afternoon, Mel sat inside the luxurious spa atmosphere of Belle Journèe salon as Lilly's stylist, Marguerite, snipped and measured what seemed like each strand of hair on Mel's head. Snipped and measured again, over and over with precise little moves.

She and Adam had arrived an hour prior, and the slender stylist had pulled Mel into the back immediately to start her transformation.

Prior to cutting, Marguerite had painted tiny strips of color onto the front and sides of Mel's hair, then carefully wrapped each strip in foil, leaving shiny multicolored tabs sticking up all over her head. Highlights, she'd been informed.

Now the stylist moved back and forth, from one side of Mel's chair to the other, their expression brimming with concentration. Marguerite wore all black—leggings, turtleneck, and smock—their hair in a bright-turquoise-and-pink fauxhawk with full makeup to match. Marguerite was transgender and quite possibly one of the most beautiful people Mel had ever seen. Plus, with all the stylist's well-placed piercings, Mel was seriously considering getting more than just her ears pierced. She turned slightly to admire the tiny diamond stud glinting from Marguerite's right nostril and another through their left eyebrow, and wondered if she should shake things up even more in her makeover.

"If you keep moving, honey, I can't be responsible for the accuracy of your cut," Marguerite said, giving Mel a stern stare in the mirror. "I pride myself on accuracy, among other things."

Mel stilled immediately, staring in the reflection to where Adam sat alone in the waiting area, looking as out of place as a priest in purgatory. Lilly had cancelled at the last minute, leaving the two of them on their own. Mel just hoped whatever magic had made Adam suddenly change his mind and agree to help her continued until their August deadline.

"Almost done." Marguerite swiveled the chair slightly, so Mel couldn't see in the mirror any longer. "Sit back, relax, and get ready for your big reveal."

Her stomach knotted. The anticipation was killing her. She turned slightly and received another temperamental grunt from Marguerite and a firm hand on either side of her head, forcing it front again.

Finally, after what seemed an eternity, the stylist stopped working and hauled Mel over to the shampoo area. Her hair was washed and rinsed to within an inch of its life, and all those tiny foils were removed. Then a towel was draped over her head, again preventing her from seeing anything as she was led back to the stylist's station, where Marguerite blow-dried and fluffed her new do.

At last, the stylist stepped back and gave Mel a beaming smile. "I have outdone myself this time, honey. You are magnificent."

Mel's chair was turned slowly to face the mirror and... *Wow!*

What a difference a cut and color made. Where her hair had been uniformly dark before, now there were shimmering highlights of caramel and auburn and even blond running through it. There were layers, too, around her face and through the crown, adding much-needed volume. She wasn't club-ready yet, given her lack of makeup, but she was closer than when she'd walked in.

Then Marguerite went to fetch the tools for the next part of the makeover, and Mel glanced up to find Adam approaching, the look on his face an odd mix of wariness and wonder. Her heart tripped. Not exactly overwhelming enthusiasm for her new look, but not outright dislike, either. He seemed a bit astonished by her new haircut, actually, as he stopped beside her chair, staring.

"I like it," she said defensively, his prolonged silence making her feel awkward. "A lot."

Adam seemed to find his voice at last, his words emerging low and filled with surprise. "It's... good, Mel. Brings out your eyes."

The tightness her chest melted into warm goo as Marguerite returned with a plastic makeup caddy filled with brushes and tubes and pots of color, similar to what Lilly had brought over the other night. The stylist turned to Adam and hiked a thumb at the empty chair at the next station. "Have a seat."

Soon, Mel's face was patted with powders and gels and concealers. While that set, Marguerite tweezed Mel's eyebrows. "Honey, you have beautiful skin. You don't need a lot of foundation or touch-up. We want to enhance, not cover you up. A little goes a long way."

Mel noted the colors Marguerite used—sparkly peach blush, coppery eye shadow, black eyeliner and mascara, a pinkish nude lip stain. Adam sat at the station across from her, staring at the toes of his boots. Or maybe he'd fallen asleep. It was hard to tell since time had gone off-kilter in this place.

"Done!" Marguerite stepped back at last, and Mel locked eyes with her transformed self for the second time, not quite believing what she saw reflected in the mirror. Where Lilly's makeup the other night had felt foreign, like paint, this felt natural, normal. Mel touched her face, then the soft wisps of hair around her face. Adam had been right. The new highlights did bring out her eyes. It was Mel, improved. Looking professional, confident, and more than a tad bit sexy.

Okay. A whole lot sexy.

"Is it really me?" she whispered.

"It is." Adam stood and moved in beside her chair, his face flushed as he ran a finger beneath the collar of his black T-shirt.

"Okay, kiddos," Marguerite said before either of them could say anything else. They held a white handled shopping bag to Mel. "Free goodies for you. Samples of everything I used today. Should last you for a month or more. By the time you run out, you'll be due back to see me for a touch-up." The stylist winked. "You're drop-dead gorgeous, honey. Hold your head high and be awesome."

She and Adam were herded toward the front entrance before Mel dug in her heels. "Wait! I need to pay."

"Lilly already took care of it," Marguerite said. "Her treat, she said. Now you lovebirds enjoy the rest of your day. I've got my next client waiting."

"Oh, we're not—" Mel and Adam said in unison, but Marguerite was already gone, moving away to greet their next client in the waiting area.

"So." Mel said as she stepped out of the path of all the people walking past them in the busy mall concourse, sunlight streaming in from the skylights above. From somewhere in the distance the sound of a fountain gurgled. "Where to from here?"

Adam continued to watch her, as if seeing her for the first time. "Marguerite was right. You're gorgeous, Mel."

She couldn't help fidgeting under his intense scrutiny. The warm fuzziness that had filled her earlier now turned molten, spreading need outward from her core to her extremities. Self-consciously, she tucked her hair behind her ear, realizing how much lighter and softer it felt. "Thanks. I really love what Marguerite did."

Adam brushed his fingertips over her forehead, tracing her widow's peak. "It suits you. You have a heart-shaped face."

"Since when do you know about women's face shapes?"

He dropped his hand and looked away then, clearing his throat. "I don't. Not sure why I said that."

But something deep inside Mel told her he was lying. He knew why'd he'd said it. Funny, but after all those years of fantasizing about him finally noticing her as a woman, all it took was a haircut.

Adam continued to study a potted plant beside him like it was the most interesting thing he'd ever seen as he dug the toe of his boot into the tile floor. "You hungry?"

Mel had to remind herself that this wasn't a date. Adam might think she was attractive now, but that was all. They'd made a deal. He'd been clear—no dating, no sex. So, yeah, lunch sounded perfect because that was all she was going to get with him. They'd chat, relax, recalibrate, then shop for a new wardrobe. She wasn't actually looking forward to seeing herself in the unforgiving dressing room mirrors, but she wanted his opinion on the clothes, so...

She forced a confident smile and started off toward the restaurants in the mall. "I am. Let's go to Cheesecake Factory. I'm buying."

ADAM COULDN'T SEEM to quit glancing at Mel as they waited in line for a table at the popular eatery. Maybe it was seeing her with new hair and a new look that had changed things—made Mel more than a girl he'd known half his life, a girl he'd laughed with and consoled when she cried, a girl he'd played stupid video games with until the wee hours.

Or maybe it was being in a different location, one where no one knew them and they could just be themselves, without all the baggage.

Whatever it was, Adam had finally been forced to acknowledge that he found Mel attractive as a woman. Seeing her after her reveal in the salon had made all his senses sit up and beg.

Even now, her nearness had his body tightening with awareness.

This was going to be a problem. But Adam was a man of his word. A promise was a promise. It was what had gotten him through his tours of duty, and it was what would get him through this new minefield with Mel. He'd vowed to help her with this crazy scheme, and he'd protect her through it, come what may.

He'd keep his hands, and his heart, to himself.

The hostess called their name and escorted them through the packed house to a large booth near the windows in the back; Adam did his best not to notice the sway of Mel's hips as she walked in front of him or the unsteady trip of his own heart.

They took seats on opposite sides of the booth, and Adam took refuge behind his massive menu while Mel chatted away about her books and her library and her time in the salon. He made occasional grunts or murmurs to show he was paying attention, but in truth, his mind was nothing but grinding gears. He'd thought Mel was beautiful before the haircut and makeup. But seeing her now taken the turmoil inside him to a whole new level. All of it had combined to smack him over the head like a sledgehammer. He felt off-balance and shaky and decidedly unsure about where to go from here.

But the thing that kept him from running, that made his skin crawl with anxiety, was if he didn't help her, some other guy would. Some guy who may not have Mel's best interests at heart. So he sat in an overpriced restaurant with a twenty-five-page menu and quite possibly the most massive slabs of cheesecake he'd ever seen, feeling more like he was facing the firing squad than helping out a friend.

"What are you going to have?" Mel asked, smiling at him over the top of her menu.

Adam shrugged. "Probably a burger, same as always."

"Break out of your comfort zone." She grinned. "I am."

Food wasn't something Adam thought a lot about. As long as his belly was full, he was good. In the military, you wolfed down whatever they served you in record time because you never knew when you might get called out to the field. Now that he was back stateside, he pretty much stuck to the basics. Living alone meant cooking for one, which wasn't fun. Not that he knew how to make much anyway. Mac and cheese from a box. Scrambled eggs. A steak or burger on the grill. That was about it.

He flipped through the pages of his menu again, frowning at all the offerings. "I don't even know what half this stuff is. What do you recommend?"

"I'm having truffle honey chicken with asparagus and mashed potatoes." Mel set her menu aside. "And cheesecake for dessert, of course."

A waiter walked by with a tray full of food, and Adam sniffed the delicious aromas of garlic and caramelized onions. "I wonder what that is."

"Ask the server when they come," Mel suggested.

Adam did that, finding out it was something called Carne Asada Steak Medallions. He'd never had them, but he liked Mexican food, he so gave them a try. Mel placed her order too, and their drinks arrived shortly thereafter. Iced tea for Mel and a Bud Light in the bottle for Adam. A man needed all the fortitude he could get for clothes-shopping.

Thankfully, Mel carried the conversation for them both,

gossiping about people around Point Beacon she'd run into through the library. Who was getting married, who was getting divorced, who was cheating on whom. Adam had never really thought being a librarian would be that exciting, but the way Mel talked about it, it sounded like the coolest job ever.

Well, besides being a mechanic. He did love his Victory Vets.

He'd noticed that since they'd left the salon there'd been a change in Mel. He wasn't sure she was even aware of it yet herself, but he hadn't missed the looks she'd gotten from people in the restaurant as they'd been led to their table. Not because he was being possessive. She wanted to change her life, and he was here to make sure it happened, safely. Mel was his to protect during the process, that was all.

Liar.

Well, regardless, he was sticking with what he knew where Mel was concerned. He'd deal with his weird new feelings and he'd move on when it was over because that was the deal. He wouldn't ruin her chances of finding love and happiness by letting her get involved with a dead-end, nowhere guy like him, even if she did look at him sometimes like he was one of those slabs of scrumptious cheesecake.

Speaking of scrumptious, that word led to all sorts of forbidden images of the two of them together in his bed, with whipped cream and caramel sauce, feeding each other bites of dessert before forgetting about the food altogether and...

Do. Not. Go. There.

He closed his eyes and scrubbed his hand over his face, glad when the waiter returned with their first courses—a salad for him and soup for her.

"Can I get either of you anything else right now?" the server asked.

"No, thanks," Mel said.

She smiled, and it felt like the clouds parted and the day brightened for Adam. Which only made him grumpier because he didn't want his world coming to life when Mel was around. They were partners on her quest to change herself. That's all. He needed to stay businesslike, unemotional, unattached to her.

He dug into his food rather than think about that anymore. The crisp veggies in his house salad were surprisingly good, as was the ranch dressing he smothered them in. Adam worked out pretty regularly at home, plus all the heavy lifting and moving in the garage, so he could eat whatever he wanted, within reason. He grabbed a breadstick from the basket between them and bit into it, looking over at Mel to find her watching him.

"What?" he asked around a mouthful of food.

"Nothing." She shook her head and sipped her soup, all dainty and ladylike. "It's good to hang out with you again is all. I've missed you."

"Yeah?" He lowered his gaze. He'd missed her, too. He hadn't realized how much until they were back together again. "How's the soup?"

"Good." She dabbed her mouth with her napkin, then gave a delighted squeal that made certain parts of him sit up and take notice. "Look, the lip stain doesn't wipe off. That is so cool."

Adam nodded and looked away fast, his cheeks prickling with guilty heat, because now all he could picture was him kissing her long enough to really test out how well that new makeup of hers lasted.

Mel sighed after a while, tucking her napkin back onto her lap. "Look, I know this is difficult for you, and I hope you know how grateful I am that you're helping me, Adam."

He came up with an answer that wasn't a total lie. "I do, Mel. It's just awkward sometimes. This isn't exactly my usual MO. Fancy eats and designer clothes and stuff. I'm a jeans and barbecue kind of guy."

"How will your bad-boy image ever survive an afternoon of clothes shopping?" she asked, using a fake Southern drawl like Scarlett O'Hara, complete with a wrist to her forehead like she was going to faint.

It was supposed to be funny, but his struggle was real. He'd figured bringing her here would be easy, drinking fancy bottled water and looking at hot chicks in magazines while he waited for her at the salon and shops. But now that he knew Mel expected him to actively participate in all of it, that meant spending even more time together in close quarters.

Adam tried to play things off by devouring the rest of his salad and breadstick before the waiter returned to clear their dishes.

Keeping on the straight and narrow, he returned to military analogies to deal with the shopping ahead. "What's your plan of attack? Any particular stores you want to target?"

Her green eyes sparkled as she talked about the places in this exclusive little mall. She rattled off several names, but they didn't mean squat to Adam, nor did he really care. Not with the way her hair danced around her face when she moved. Not with the sweetness of her grin that warmed him from the inside out. He wasn't sure how he'd let Mel go at the end of all this, only that he would. Because of who she was and what he wasn't.

When he focused the conversation again, Mel watched him expectantly as if waiting for an answer. *Crap.* He had no idea what she'd said. His head pounded and his heart raced and if he didn't come up with something quick, he was liable to lean across the table and kiss her until neither of them cared about clothes anymore. So he said, "Fine."

"Wow," Mel said. "The shoes, too?"

"Huh?" That must've been what she'd asked him. Something about shoes.

The waiter returned with their main courses, and they both sat back. As Adam stared at his plate of steak and peppers and the delectable smell of onions drifted around him, he knew it didn't matter what she wanted to do, within reason, because he was going to say yes.

Maybe it wouldn't be so bad. After all, he'd tried something new with his meal choice and, from the looks of it, it would be amazing. So maybe going with the flow with Mel this afternoon would work out okay, too.

He gave her a tentative smile and picked up his knife and fork. "Shoes, too."

"Great." Mel dug into her chicken and veggies, glancing his way periodically as if she wanted to ask him something but wasn't sure how. Finally, she came out with it. "So, what was it like? Being deployed overseas?"

He shrugged, hoping she'd drop the subject. Talking about the war wasn't his favorite topic. Especially today, when it was supposed to be all about her and light and fun.

During his service, sunny, fun spots had been few and far between.

Mel persisted though. "I've tried to ask James, but he never wants to talk about it. I've read some horror stories online."

Adam took a deep breath. There was a reason most of the guys didn't discuss what happened on deployments afterward. It was tough to verbalize to someone else what you could barely wrap your head around yourself. Still, Mel was staring at him again with those pretty eyes, so he felt like he should try. They had a whole afternoon filled with conversation stretching ahead of them. Maybe if he opened up to her a little now, she wouldn't press him for more later. "I don't know. It was weird. It's still weird, being home."

"Weird how?"

"Like I enlisted to be a good citizen and do my duty. It wasn't like I had a lot going on around here anyway." He swallowed another bite of food, then took a sip of his beer before continuing. "College wasn't an option for me. No money for it and my grades weren't good enough for scholarships or grants. Plus, I had no real family life, so yeah. I joined up. Figured I'd go over there, help make things better, hopefully come home with all my limbs and my mind intact, learn how to be a leader or learn a new trade, become someone I could be proud of."

"And did you?" she asked, tilting her head to the side, her expression thoughtful. "Learn how to be a leader? Become someone you were proud of?"

"Yes and no." He stared out the window near their table, at the people milling about in the parking lot. "I gained a stronger identity being on my own. I wasn't just the town delinquent anymore, the local screwup. Going overseas gave me the rare opportunity to reinvent myself, to become the man I wanted to be. In that respect, I guess it was a good experience. I became stronger, braver, better able to stand up for myself and what I believed in. So yeah, I guess I was successful in that sense."

Mel pushed her half-finished plate aside. "But not in others?"

"No, not in others. To be honest, deployment was really confusing." Adam looked back at her, finding himself wanting to tell her things he hadn't ever wanted to tell anyone else. But here, in their little corner of the restaurant, he felt safe enough to open up. He sat back as the waiter cleared their plates and took their cheesecake order.

Once they were alone again, he continued. "When they first send you into battle, after basic training, they tell you you're going to fight the enemy. But the thing is, there's no way to tell who's the enemy and who isn't when you're there. It's not like they wore buttons or anything. Like one day you roll into a village on a humanitarian visit and these people bring their kids into the clinic you helped set up for treatment, then the next day they're shooting at you. What's worse is a lot of them didn't even know why we were there. They live in remote areas with no connection to the outside world. They'd never heard of 9/11 or Americans coming or whatever. Plus, there are tons of regional dialects in these places too, so even if you learn the basics of the language, communication is a problem."

"That sounds really hard." Mel's feet brushed his under the table before she pulled back again. "It makes sense now why James doesn't want to talk about it."

"Sorry to put a damper on the mood," he said, kicking himself for not just coming up with some convenient lie instead of spilling the ugly truth. In an effort to get back to the light easiness of before, he added, "It wasn't all horrible, though."

"Yeah?" Her small smile lifted his spirits and made the shadows recede. Or maybe that was the waiter returned with their dessert. "Tell me."

"Back when I learned about the Middle East in Mr. Knudten's geography class I thought the whole place was sand and mountains." He snuck a bite of his chocolate hazelnut cheesecake and, man, it definitely lived up to the hype. "Anyway, it's not all like that. I probably spent as much time in orchards as I did anyplace else. One time we hiked through a jungle. Then it rained for days and we had to dig irrigation trenches because of flooding in our camp. Definitely not all arid sand and mountains."

She nodded, trying a bite of her cinnamon swirl cheesecake as the waiter returned with their check. "What else surprised you in a good way?"

"Food sharing is a big part of the culture there." He snagged the check before she could and pulled his wallet from his back pocket before Mel could object. "If anyone has something to eat, custom says you have to share it with everyone. Even if you only brought a little. People get, like, really offended if you eat in front of them and don't offer them any. Gives family-style dining a whole new meaning."

"So you're saying the next time we eat together we should share a plate to make things easier, is that right?"

Her coy little grin made the warmth inside him kick up a notch. The thought of sharing a plate with her, of feeding her, of tasting the spicy flavors in her kisses...

Adam gulped his water to drown those erotic images before answering. "Maybe we should just start with our cheesecake."

She snuck a bite of his dessert while Adam took care of the credit card receipt from the waiter, glad for the distraction.

"Here, try a bite of mine, too," she said, holding out her fork to him with a bite of her dessert on it once they were alone again. Without much choice, Adam leaned forward. Mel placed the bite of cheesecake on his tongue, all creamy and smooth and spicy from the cinnamon. He chewed fast before swallowing, as much to stifle his groan of frustration as anything else.

Yep. Time to go.

He slid out of the booth then waited for Mel to do the same. "Uh, we should probably get a move on if you want to visit all those stores before we head home."

She blinked up at him a moment, close enough for her to turn slightly and kiss him on the cheek. "You deserve every good thing in life, Adam Foster. You always did. Remember that, okay?"

She then she grabbed her purse and headed for the exit, leaving him behind to stare after her as she called, "Let's hit those stores."

CHAPTER SIX

"I think maybe we should try someplace else," Mel said, looking around the trendy boutique she'd wanted to visit. It was packed to the shiny mirrored ceiling with pants and tops and skirts and sweaters in an array of fashionable hues straight out of the latest style magazines she read on her breaks at the library. Everything looked expensive and adorable and way too intimidating for Mel to even touch. "I doubt these will fit."

"What? Don't be silly." Adam took her hand and tugged her forward, giving her a side-glance once-over that had her toes curling in her sandals. "These will fit you. Trust me."

He stood to the side while she carefully flipped through the racks, pulling things out and draping them over her arm. She smiled benignly at the sales staff milling about, praying they wouldn't approach. The staff all looked perfect and polished and would no doubt find Mel lacking in the worst way. Finally, they moved toward the dressing rooms at the back of the store with her armload of garments.

"May I help you with those?" a salesclerk interceded before they reached their destination, probably sensing a sizable commission, though her tone seemed sincere. She unlocked one of the dressing rooms, then helped Mel hang everything on the hooks inside. "My name's Andi, and I'll be outside if you need anything. Let me know."

Adam took up guard position beside the door, while Mel locked herself inside, shaking her head. "I'm telling you, none of this stuff will fit."

"How do you know?" he asked. You haven't even tried any of it on yet. I bet it'll fit you just fine."

"If you're right and I even half this stuff works for me, then I owe you a beer."

He chuckled. "Okay. And what do I owe you if I'm wrong?"

The slight flirtation in his tone made her pulse thud.

A kiss.

The words teetered on the edge of her lips, but she chickened out. "I don't know."

"Hmm," he said, sounding skeptical. "Hurry up and change."

She stared at all the clothes on the hooks. Since high school, she'd worn the same style, the same size. She knew what worked for her and what didn't. Handing him back all this stuff after she was done and making him take her to a different store because she'd been right after all would be sweet revenge. Those thoughts finally spurred her to undress.

"How's it going in there?" Adam called a short time later.

"Dandy." Mel pulled a pair of skinny jeans off a hanger and tugged them on. "Give me a minute."

"You've had five already. Not that I'm counting or anything."

Mel sighed, picturing him leaning against the wall, looking effortlessly gorgeous and drawing all sorts of female attention without even trying. He'd always been far too sexy for his own good.

Surprisingly, the jeans slid up her legs and over her butt with ease, like they were made for her. She buttoned and zipped them, then turned looked in the mirror, her mouth agape. They fit her like a second skin, in a good way. That couldn't be right.

Mel checked all the angles and found nothing amiss. No muffin top, no pinching, nothing but a perfect fit.

Adam knocked on the door again. "Are you stalling because you owe me a Bud Light?"

"Maybe."

His arrogant chuckle had her grabbing a light blue top off another hanger, the fabric a silky rayon jersey with a cowl neck and cap sleeves. A far cry from her usual twinsets and pearls. She pulled it over her head, then wriggled it down to her waist. The clingy material hugged her curves without being too revealing, and the color made her skin glow. After one last check in the mirror, she reached for the door handle, needing confirmation that she wasn't imagining all this.

"All bets are off until you let me see..." Adam's words trailed off as she opened the door. He stood frozen, his gaze moving slowly upward from her bare toes, over her hips and thighs to her chest. Mel had long since stopped breathing. Time seemed to slow. No, she wasn't imagining it at all.

Each flicker of his gaze over her felt like warm honey on her skin, slow and sweet and delicious. Adam swallowed hard, the muscles working in his strong, tanned neck working, and Mel had the sudden urge to nuzzle the hollow at the base of his throat.

She vowed then to buy this outfit and wear it whenever he was around.

When he spoke, his voice sounded rougher than before. "Told you they'd fit."

"Guess I owe you a beer then." Mel crossed her arms, the move thrusting her boobs up higher. His attention returned to her chest and her pulse tripped. She uncrossed them and smoothed her hands down her sides instead.

"Good thing, because I could use a drink." His husky, self-deprecating response was the sexiest thing Mel had ever heard, and she rested a hand against the wall for support.

"Since when did you become an expert on women's clothes?" Mel asked, desperate to distract herself before she tackled him to the marble floor of the boutique and kissed him silly. "Most guys wouldn't know a cute top from a turnip."

Her words seemed to finally break him out of his daze. Adam turned away, but not before she caught the heat in his eyes. "I spend a lot of time around females. I pay attention to what they like."

"I bet you do." She shifted her weight. His experience was why she'd wanted his help, right? The fact that it bothered her now made no sense whatsoever.

Adam rubbed the back of his neck, his hand shaking slightly. And now her heart ached for an entirely different reason—tenderness. Apparently, the bad boy of Point Beacon was as affected by her as she was by him.

She savored his reactions a bit longer as she glanced back into the dressing room mirror again, moving this way and that to see all her angles. "You're sure this outfit isn't too tight?"

"No." His voice sounded strained as he licked his lips. She met his gaze in the mirror, and the air between them seemed to sizzle. Then he stepped forward to nudge her back inside the dressing room. "It looks great. You look great. Trust me."

He was standing so close now. Mel closed her eyes and swayed toward him before she could stop herself, her forehead bumping his chin.

"Please, Mel," Adam growled, the sound tight with tension. "Try on the rest. Pick out a few that you like and let's go."

He then left, shutting the door behind him. Mel wondered when things had gotten so crazy. She also wondered what she'd have to do to make him lose his control and finally kiss her.

"I answered your questions back at the restaurant about my service," he said after a while through the door. "Now it's your turn to tell me something in exchange?"

"Like what?" Mel asked, not liking where this could go.

"Tell me what you're looking for in a boyfriend."

You.

She slumped against the wall of the dressing room, eyes closed, forcing herself to answer. "I want someone who's smart and funny and kind and sweet. Someone who makes me laugh and makes me feel protected and cherished. A person who's loyal and honest and steadfast. Who won't run at the first hint of trouble. It would be nice if he had a great smile and beautiful eyes, too."

Like you.

"That's a tall order," Adam said after a moment. "Not sure we can find a guy like that."

Mel straightened and slipped her feet into her shoes.

This new outfit was comfortable, and after Adam's reaction, they'd have to pry the clothes off her cold dead body. She was wearing them home. As she packed up her other clothes, she said, "Well, if we can tick most of those boxes, we're good."

After the way he'd shared with her at the restaurant and how great he'd been today, she felt like she was finally on the right track with him. They'd part ways, still friends, on her birthday. Until then, though, she still had a few more weeks, a few more chances to break down his walls and get him to open up to her and see how great they could be together.

ADAM HAD STARTED today's adventure with a positive attitude, but now it was fading fast. Not that he hadn't enjoyed the time with Mel. On the contrary, he'd enjoyed it too much. That was the problem.

He kept his eyes straight ahead as he drove Mel's Camry back toward Point Beacon, merging onto the exit ramp from Interstate 465 to 69 North, willing his inappropriate attraction to her back into submission. Each time he closed his eyes, he could still see her looking at him with those big green eyes, could still feel every time she'd brushed again him, the way she looked, her scent. Everything she did seemed to be a natural aphrodisiac where he was concerned.

And if he couldn't resist her, what about the rest of the male population in their zip code?

He'd been so distracted by her that he hadn't even thought of his business all day. What kind of owner did that make him?

A messed-up, horny one. That's what.

Adam glanced at the speedometer and realized he was going well over the speed limit and eased up on the accelerator. They'd left the mall an hour ago, and he was still thinking about the way Mel's butt looked in those jeans—even though her nonstop chatter from the passenger seat should've doused his lust like a fire extinguisher on the ride home.

He sighed and shifted in his seat, staring out at the endless farm fields surrounding them. After he dropped her off at her place, he planned to get on his bike and ride for a few hours, forget about that promised beer she owed him. Because accepting it meant more time with Mel. In her house. Alone.

And yeah, Adam liked to live on the edge as much as the next hellion, but this was insane. The miles flew past until the Welcome to Point Beacon sign showed in his headlights just after sundown. He pulled into Mel's driveway a few minutes later and parked. Mel got out and walked around to the trunk. He followed, his Harley mocking him from the side of her garage where he'd parked it this morning. For a crazy second, he considered making a break for it and hurtling away at breakneck speed, but that idea was soon nixed as Mel handed him bag after bag from her shopping spree.

The last lingering streaks of violet were fading in the indigo sky. A warm breeze stirred but did little to cool Adam's overheated body. The weight he carried didn't keep him from watching the sway of Mel's hips again as she walked up the steps to her front door. Man, those jeans were going to kill him one of these days.

She smiled at him over her shoulder as she unlocked the door. "Excuse the mess, please."

She'd mentioned that the first time he'd been over, too, but her place was neat as a pin, far as he could see. Compared to his home, it looked like the frigging Taj Mahal. She went inside, putting out a foot to keep that fluffy cat of hers from escaping as she flipped on the lights. Adam put her bags on the sofa in the living room, per her direction, then glanced over at the coffee table, where a copy of the *Cosmo* sex guide sat, several tabs marking the pages. He swallowed hard.

"How about the beer I owe you?" Mel called from the kitchen.

"Uh, actually I should probably go," he called, rushing back toward the foyer like his butt was on fire.

"I'm sorry?" she said, coming down the hall toward him. "I didn't hear you."

She'd already pulled two Bud Lights from her fridge and twisted the caps off. He stood, torn, as she passed him a bottle. He hated to waste a good beer.

Mel drank hers, nose wrinkled. He wondered why she'd bought these when she clearly didn't like them, but feared he already knew the answer. She shrugged. "Wine's more my thing."

Adam nodded, sipping for his own bottle as he searched for some topic of conversation. His brain landed on the bar the other night. "Uh, Lilly and Dom seem pretty solid."

"Yeah. They've been together a whole month. New record, I think." Mel leaned against the doorframe leading into the living room. She'd taken off her shoes, he noticed. Her pink polished toes sticking out from beneath the hem of her jeans. "Seems like she might have met her match."

Her voice went soft when she said that, as did her eyes, and something pulled taut inside Adam, sending a pang of yearning deep into his chest. He found himself moving closer to Mel before he could stop himself. Close enough that if he reached out, he could pull Mel closer for the kiss he'd been dying to give her all day.

Mel tilted her head and squinted at him. "Are you okay? You got awfully quiet."

"Lots on my mind. Garage stuff." He lied through his teeth. "I really should go."

He stepped back, careful not to make any more bodily contact.

"Guess I'll see you next time," she said, one eyebrow raised. "You'll call me to set up the next lesson, right?"

"Right." Somewhere between the clothes and the shoes and the lunch and the lust that afternoon, he'd lost control of this entire situation. He couldn't say exactly when or why, but he blamed the pheromone-fueled fog in his brain that worsened whenever Mel was around.

He'd almost reached the front door when her cat twined around his ankles, nearly tripping him. Adam caught himself against the wall and did his best to disentangle himself from the frisky feline.

Mel bent and picked up her cat, kissing its head, then cuddled it under her chin.

Lucky cat.

"I'll call you, I promise," he said, one hand on the doorknob.

"I'll be waiting, as usual." She sounded so forlorn, his

couldn't stop himself from slipping his fingers beneath her chin, forcing her to meet his gaze.

"Hey. Don't talk like that."

At his touch, she inhaled, drawing his attention to her chest again in that slinky blue top. As if drawn by some invisible tractor beam, Adam leaned in and brushed his lips over hers, so lightly they were hardly there at all. Mel's mouth moved beneath his, sweet and soft, just like he imagined, and he drew back before he couldn't anymore.

"Talk to you soon," Adam said, then rushed into the warm summer night.

CHAPTER SEVEN

The next morning, Mel's nerves were shot.

As she stood behind the circulation desk at Point Beacon Public Library going over the list of books she needed to pull that day for storage to make room for the new titles coming in, she pasted on a smile and vowed to get through it. Even if her new outfit felt like a big arrow pointing her out for all to see.

Truthfully, other than a few side glances from her elderly volunteers, no one had made a comment about her new clothing choices. Then again, most of the patrons that day were too focused on getting to their small genealogy section before it filled to capacity. Seemed tracing one's family tree was a hot new trend in Point Beacon. Most people went online to search, but these patrons were all from the retirement center across town, and Mel doubted they had the technology resources in their community.

Besides, she was determined to see her plan through and prove to herself she could do this. Head high and shoulders back, she moved out from behind the desk and headed to the nonfiction section to locate a biography on James Dean an internet patron had put a hold on for future pickup.

Speaking of future pickups...

Each time she closed her eyes, she could still feel Adam's lips on hers, his breath warm, the taste of alcohol and desire in his mouth. Talk about the stuff fantasies were made of. In all her years of pining for the guy, nothing beat the first real thing. He'd smelled of soap and sandalwood and a hint motor oil and she'd felt like she was flying, so high in the clouds she'd lost touch with reality for a second.

Then Adam had bolted through the door, muttering an apology. To him, apparently, the kiss had been a mistake, an error in judgment.

Until she could prove to him otherwise, she had to tread lightly.

She tugged at the hem of her new fitted black top, then crouched to pull the biography from the bottom shelf. Even she had to admit the new black pants she'd worn made life much easier. She'd been caught in a rut of her own making, she realized. Perhaps it was time to stop sticking to the status quo in other areas too.

Retrieved book in hand, she straightened and glimpsed her reflection in the glass front of a memorabilia case lining the wall nearby. She'd made her first attempt at re-creating Marguerite's genius on her hair that morning, and though it wasn't quite as perfect as it had been in the salon, it still looked good. Her makeup did too. She'd applied with a light hand, as the stylist had suggested, and she looked well rested and refreshed, if not *Vogue* cover-worthy.

Which was surprising since she'd slept like crap last night.

Kissing the man of your dreams only to have him flee afterward did that to a girl.

Mel headed back to the circulation desk as the automatic doors near the entrance swished open and in walked her mother, carrying an armload of library books Mel suspected were overdue.

While Mel and her mom were similar heights and weights, that's where the similarities ended. Audrey Bryant was a force to be reckoned with around Point Beacon. Along with Mel's father, Bud, they were the cool parents every kid wished they'd had. Mel had always balked when Lilly told her how lucky she was to have parents like Audrey and Bud. Not that Mel didn't love her mom and dad. She did, but that wasn't the issue. The issue was they were too close to see what was right in front of them. Like James being gay. Or Mel being in love with Adam Foster.

"Morning, dear." Her mother dumped her load on the desktop, then straightened the designer purse slung over her shoulder. "We missed you last night."

"Sorry." Mel averted her gaze as she stacked and sorted the items her mother had returned. Friday evenings at her parents' house were game night, but she didn't regret her choice to spend it with Adam instead. Not that she'd tell her mother that. She shook her head and grabbed another tome to scan back into the library's inventory. "I had to go out of town yesterday and didn't get back until late."

"Where?" Her mom's voice perked up. "A conference?"

"No. Personal errand." Not the whole truth, but not a lie either.

"And you got your hair cut!" Her mother's excitement echoed in the quiet library and drew the attention—and scowls —of several nearby senior citizens. Her mom cringed and flashed Mel a conciliatory smile. "Sorry. It's just been so long, and I love it! The highlights really suit your skin tone. Good for you, dear."

Heat prickled Mel's cheeks as she moved to put the books in the bin to be resolved. Surprisingly, none of them were overdue. The Bryant clan weren't known for their excellent timing.

"Thanks." Mel said. "I went to the same stylist Lilly does in Indy. Got my makeup done too and did a bit of shopping afterward."

"I see that." Her mom grinned. "Lilly went with you then?"

"Uh, yeah." Mel's skin prickled from the lie, but she could hardly tell her mother the truth at this point. It would ruin everything.

"Huh. That's weird. I ran into her earlier at the grocery store and she didn't mention anything." Flustered, Mel opened her mouth to answer then closed it again. Thankfully, her mother moved on to other topics. "Anyway, I came to remind you of dinner tomorrow."

Mel hovered between relief and nausea. It was one thing to avoid detection in brief interactions. Quite another to sit for several hours and be grilled across the dining room table. But then she really couldn't cancel now without drawing more suspicion, so she bit the bullet and asked, "What time?"

"One. Same as always." Her mom glanced through a pile of returned books stacked up near the overnight slot. "Oh, and guess who else I ran into at the grocery?"

The question, innocent enough on its own, sent a spike of

apprehension though Mel. She swallowed hard as she scanned in the bar code for the requested James Dean biography and typed in the reserved date beside the requesting patron's name on her computer screen. "Who?"

"Adam Foster. I've been meaning to stop by Victory Vets and say hello to him since he returned to town, but it's been so crazy volunteering for the town art council that time got away from me. Anyway, I invited him for dinner tomorrow too."

Mel's heart stuttered. "What?"

"He tried to get out of it, of course," her mother continued. But I told him I'd make the pot roast he loves so much. Said it would be like old times and refused to take no for an answer." Her mom patted Mel's hand. "And he said he can't wait to see you too. I wonder if he's dating anyone. I should set him up with that nice gal from the diner who just moved to town a few months back. What do you think?"

"I think you should let Adam have his privacy," Mel said, the words stilted by the vise-like tension squeezing her chest tighter by the second. Mel gathered up the bin of returns, then backed away slowly. "I appreciate you returning the books, Mom, but I really need to get back to work. The weekly book club meets this afternoon, and I have to prepare the question-and-answer section. Then there's the discussion group to lead tonight for the history club. I'll see you at dinner tomorrow, yeah?"

Her mom gave her an odd look, then turned on her heel and headed for the exit. "Fine, dear. See you then. It'll be fun."

Fun.

Not exactly the first word that popped into Mel's mind for what was sure to be a disaster tomorrow. All sorts of nightmare scenarios ran through her head. What if Adam blurted out their little plan in front of her parents? What if they picked up on something weird between them? What if Mel couldn't control herself and kissed Adam silly on her parents' sofa?

The horrific anxiety plagued her the rest of the day and all through the night, raising Mel's stress levels to unbearable by the time Sunday rolled around.

She stood before her closet, unable to decide what to wear.

She tried on the jeans and blue top, then quickly discarded them. A reminder of her brief kiss with Adam, followed by him running for the hills. Next, she considered wearing the black top and pants from the day before again. But they quickly joined the growing pile of rejects atop the bed. Too stuffy and businesslike. The last thing she wanted was for Adam to think she'd given up one kind of armor for another. She wanted to project an image of relaxed confidence now. It was Sunday dinner with her family, after all. Why was she so nervous about it?

Because Adam would be there.

Which made no sense because she'd eaten meals with the guy probably a million times growing up, and she'd never seen Adam wear anything other than jeans and black T-shirts. She needed to chill.

Mel eyed the blue top and jeans again, remembering the way he'd looked at her when she'd come out of the dressing room in the boutique. Like he was a starving man and she was a banquet.

Wearing that outfit again, especially in front of her parents, was a risk, but one she was willing to take.

After rehanging the rest of the clothes she'd pulled out, Mel tugged on the jeans and slinky blue top, then checked her reflection in the full-length mirror. They still fit her like a second skin and still made her feel sexy without being too revealing. Perfect.

Next, she headed to the bathroom to do her hair and makeup. A quick glance at the clock showed it was noon. One hour to finish getting ready, then get over to her parents' house for an afternoon of food, fun, and fraud.

ADAM ROLLED his stiff neck to relieve the kink there, most likely because he'd spent the majority of the meal glancing at Mel to his right. She'd worn that blue top again, and no matter how much food he shoveled into his mouth as a distraction, he couldn't seem to keep his gaze from straying to her. Mel stood and reached for her empty plate.

Everyone else seemed to have finished eating a while ago, but Adam didn't care. He loved Mrs. Bryant's pot roast, and it was a real treat being here again. Plus, he liked looking at Mel in her new outfit and he wasn't ready to stop yet.

"Can you pass me the mashed potatoes?" he asked Mel.

She handed him the bowl as her cell phone rang on the table. "Aren't you full yet?"

He caught a glimpsed of James's name on the caller ID before she answered. Mel put the call on speaker phone, and Adam swallowed his potatoes without tasting them, his focus split between Mel's curves and the fact that his best friend was calling in from half a world away.

"Hey, bro," Mel said, flicking a glance at Adam. As nice as

dinner had been, there was still an awkward undercurrent between them after the kiss the other night. He still wasn't sure why he'd done it. And even wrong as it was, he couldn't bring himself to regret it. Not that he'd repeat it either. One and done. That was how it had to be.

"James, Adam's here too," Mrs. Bryant said, winking at him.

"Hey," Adam said. "How's the army treating you?"

"Same old, same old." James's smile was evident through the phone line. "Miss seeing you around the base. How's the business?"

"Good." Adam pushed his plate away at last. "Victory Vets picks up new customers every day. Jag and Miguel and Hollywood say hello."

"You having dinner?" James chuckled. "Still scarfing down my mom's pot roast, eh?"

"You know it." Adam rubbed his full belly. "Had thirds and fourths in your honor."

Mel had started clearing the table and leaned past Adam to grab the butter dish, bumping his shoulder with her breast. Her uneasy chuckle, combined with the searing look she gave Adam, only served to intensify the tension crackling between them. God, why had he kissed her Friday night?

A stupid rookie move. He knew better than to play with fire. And flames were definitely flaring between them now, if the sexy look she just gave him was any indication. Then, to make matters worse, Mel whispered in his ear, "You sure you've had enough?"

Time froze as he stared into her eyes, their green irises hypnotic and infinitely seductive. The rattle of glasses from the other side of the table jarred him from his inappropriate, erotic thoughts.

Get a grip, man.

Mrs. Bryant was now regaling her son with stories from Point Beacon, including his sister's new miraculous makeover. "Seriously, James. You won't recognize her when you get back. She looks like she walked out of some fashion magazine or something."

"Good for you, sis!" James said. "Glad you finally joined the twenty-first century."

Mel's cheeks flushed pink, and she tugged the neckline of her blue shirt higher. "Like you know anything about fashion."

"You tell him, kiddo. She looks great." Mr. Bryant beamed at his daughter, and Adam felt the lack of familial support even more than normal. He didn't think his own father had ever looked at him like that. Like he cared. Like his son was worth more than the dirt on his shoes.

"She reminds me more and more of your mom every day," Mr. Bryant continued.

"As long as Mel's happy, I'm happy," James said. "And she's right. I'm lucky if my socks match, let alone anything else."

Adam swallowed hard, listening in on the conversations around him. Over the years, these Sunday dinners had been the highlight of his miserable weeks. There was always lots of talk and laughs, good food and the feeling of a real home, so different from where he came from. The only place he'd imagined a world like that actually existed as a kid was in cheesy sitcoms on TV. But the Bryants proved it was real. Too bad it would all be over if they found out Adam was lying to them.

A crash sounded from the kitchen. Adam jumped and Mr.

Bryant stood. "Better go check on the ladies," he said. "I'm sure you two guys have things to talk about anyway."

He left and silence hung in the air for a moment before Adam tried to make small talk by asking James about his current mission. Last he'd heard, their platoon was providing security for a civilian village in an undisclosed location in the Middle East where a new conflict had erupted. While James told him about the false alarms and friendly fire, Adam's guilt grew because through the open doorway leading into the kitchen he could see Mel at the sink, those new jeans cupping her butt just right and all he wanted to do at that moment was put his hands there. He didn't dare though. The kiss had been bad enough. More touching would be way out of line.

James was telling him about the native interpreters and gossip from the guys at the base. Adam did his best to follow along, but he was still preoccupied with Mel.

Since Friday night, every time he closed his eyes, he pictured her against him, eyes shut and expression dreamy, her lips parted from his kiss. He'd run out of there like the coward he was, racing all the way home, praying the slap of wind on his face would drive some sense into him.

It hadn't. He'd lain awake all night, body aching. Done the same last night, too. Today had been sheer torture, having her so close and wanting her so bad, but knowing she was totally off limits.

"Why are you so quiet?" James asked suddenly, jarring Adam from his thoughts. "What's wrong?"

"Nothing's wrong." Adam cleared his throat to cover the lie. "I'm just listening to you."

"Whatever. I know when something's bothering you, so you might as well just tell me. I'll find out eventually. I always do."

And that was the problem right there. Because Adam knew he was right. He would find out. Then Adam's life would be over.

He wasn't ready for that. He wished he'd never agreed to this harebrained scheme of hers. He wished he were a better man, an honest man, but at the moment, he wasn't, couldn't be.

So, he just said, "I'm fine. Everything's fine. It's just crazy busy here without you. You better get yourself back here in one piece because we've got cars out the wazoo waiting for you to work on at the garage." He added that last part because it was true and made the lie more palatable. "And I miss you too."

Then James's next words nearly sent Adam into cardiac arrest. "It's Mel, isn't it?"

"What? No," Adam said, defensive. "Why would you say that?"

"I don't know. I've been worried about her. It's like she put her life on hold when we left and she never hit restart. I'm glad she's started changing things up again," he said. "But please tell me the truth. Is the new makeover okay?"

"Better than okay," Adam said, meaning it. "She looks great. Really beautiful."

"Beautiful huh?" James seemed to sense something in Adam's tone, making him scramble for cover.

"I mean, in an objective sort of way. Like a piece of art. Or a brand-new Harley or something."

Idiot.

James snorted. "As bad as I am at fashion, you are at art. You wouldn't know the Mona Lisa if it bit you on the butt."

"True." The observation cut through the tension building inside him and Adam laughed. "When are you coming home?"

"Not soon enough, it sounds like. Hey, will you do me a favor?" James asked. "Will you keep an eye on Mel until I get back?"

"Uh..." If he said yes to James, he'd be playing both sides, which was not a good place to be.

"I don't mean like a bodyguard or anything," James cleared. "Just watch out for her. If she's as gorgeous now as everyone tells me, she won't know how to deal with that. I just don't want her to get hurt."

I don't want that either.

"Just keep an eye out on the guys she's with. Mel doesn't have a lot of experience and I don't want her taken advantage of by the wrong sort."

Like me.

"Please?" James asked and how could Adam say no? It wasn't like he was going to date Mel anyway. They were partners on this project and that was it. And maybe he had kissed her once. He wouldn't do it again. And making this promise to James might help him keep that vow.

"Okay."

"Thanks." The relief in James's tone was obvious. "I'd hate to see her with some player like we were back in high school, right?"

"Yeah," Adam managed to squeak, past the invisible noose tightening around this neck. It was hard to breathe now, hard to sit there and pretend everything was all right, when deep down it wasn't and might never be again.

Mel walked back into the dining room then, her sunny

smile wavering at whatever she saw on Adam's face. "Every-thing okay?"

"Hey, sis. Send me a selfie of your new look please," James said, his tone even and light. "I gotta see this for myself."

"I need to go." Adam pushed to his feet. "I, uh, have some paperwork to finish up at the garage for tomorrow."

"What? You're leaving already?" Mrs. Bryant said as she returned to the dining room as well, wiping her hands on a towel. "We were going to play games."

Loneliness ached inside Adam. He'd loved game nights here, but he couldn't stay now. Not with Mel looking like his every fantasy come to life and the lies he'd just told James and his world falling apart at the seams. He backed slowly toward the front door. "Afraid so. Thanks again for dinner, Mrs. Bryant. Great seeing you all again." To James on the phone he called, "Stay safe, buddy. Can't wait to see you home next month."

"I'll walk you out," Mel said, following him to the doors.

"Uh, no." Adam stopped in his tracks. "I mean, go spend time with your family. I'll call you."

"When?" She gave him a suspicious look. "We need to talk about the going to Indy again. You said you'd take me to one of those clubs."

"At the end," he said, alarmed. "Not yet."

"I want to do some reconnaissance," she said. "Check out the clubs so I know what I'm in for and prepared, is all. Maybe we can go one night this week?"

"Oh...uh...I don't know. I'll have to check my schedule. I'll call tomorrow and let you know, I promise. Tuesday at the latest." The metal doorknob felt cold against his palm. "See you later."

With that, Adam rushed down the porch steps to the sidewalk where his bike was parked at the curb, unable to shake the fact that even thousands of miles away, James had sensed something was up with him. If that was the case, then how obvious was it to the people who saw him every day? He'd thought he'd done a good job of hiding what was happening between him and Mel, but maybe not.

As he cranked the Harley's engine, James's words reverberated in his mind.

Hate to see her end up with some player like we were back in high school...

Adam's reputation in the romance department hadn't improved much since then. He was a loser, a playboy, a bad bet. Except when he was with Mel, she made him feel like he was good enough. Made him feel like he could be a better man. Someone strong and worthy.

Someone who stuck around for the long haul, no matter what.

As he pulled away from the curb in a squeal of tires, Adam felt more torn than he'd ever been in his life. And now she wanted to go to Indy again? Worse, he was considering it. Showing her what those clubs were like wasn't a bad idea. Maybe it would show her it wasn't the glamorous thing she thought it was.

But he also didn't want to betray James, and he definitely didn't want to hurt Mel. However, since she'd said she was doing this with or without him, she was safer with him because he knew the rules.

Adam stopped at a red light and rubbed his face. Or least he'd thought he knew them, but now he wasn't so sure anymore. What scared him most was how he kept thinking about her all the time. About her laugh or her smile. Her killer body and her magnificent brain. About how she looked at him and the way she made him feel like he stood ten feet tall whenever they were together.

He couldn't remember the last time that had happened, if ever.

The light turned green, and he sped forward, trying to keep it all in perspective. It wasn't too late. It wasn't love. He just liked spending time with her, that was all. Somehow, the past week or so, Mel had gone past being James's little sister and become a vivacious woman he wanted to know better. That was all.

He'd keep it light, fun, because that's the deal he'd made.

Once this was over, he'd walk away as promised.

Because that's the only way any of this would work out in the end.

CHAPTER EIGHT

M el bit into her turkey-and-Swiss sandwich at lunch the next day, as she scrolled down a page of search engine results on her computer screen. Adam still hadn't called, but she wanted to be ready when he did. And her search for clubs in Indy had been quite interesting. There was one in particular...

The Tipsy Wench.

That's where she'd decided she wanted Adam to take her on their reconnaissance mission. Whenever that might be. He'd acted squirrelly again when he'd left her parents' house yesterday. She hadn't pressed him too hard about it because how could she with her mom and dad and James all listening in?

But after seeing the way he'd kept glancing at her butt in those jeans and how his gaze had flickered down the front of her top whenever she'd leaned over to hand him something, she knew he was definitely interested, even if he was too stubborn to admit it.

She printed off a map to the bar she'd chosen, closing the browser as the automatic doors at the library entrance swished open. She greeted the new arrival without looking up to see who'd come in. "Welcome to the Point Beacon Public Library. Please let me know if there's anything I can help you find."

"How about my sanity?" Adam said.

She looked up fast, eyes wide, forcing a nervous smile, her heart racing as it always did when he was around. Adam had never come to her library before, at least not that she remembered.

"Hey," she said, trying to sound casual. "This is a surprise. I thought you were going to call."

He shrugged, drawing her attention to his muscular torso beneath his soft dark cotton T-shirt. A bicep tattoo of the United States Army insignia peeked out from under the edge of one sleeve. Her brother had the same one, same spot, too. Dirt streaked his faded jeans, highlighting his strong thighs and trim hips. And those dark eyes. They seemed even more unfathomable, if that were possible. "Figured face-to-face was better."

Face-to-face sounded ominous. Like whatever news he had might be bad. Mel swallowed hard around the sudden lump in her throat. The room seemed warmer now as the atmosphere in the library changed from subdued to stressed. She licked her lips and didn't miss the way Adam's gaze tracked the tiny movement.

They were short a volunteer or two today, so Mel had stayed in for lunch, eating at the circulation desk to make sure they were covered for any patrons who might need help. Technically, food or drinks weren't allowed in the library, but a girl needed sustenance.

Adam glanced at her plastic containers and frowned. "Sorry. Didn't mean to interrupt."

"It's fine." She gave another look around to confirm she and Adam were alone, then asked, "What's going on?"

"We need to talk about this bar trip you want." He shuffled his feet, resting his palms on the edge of the counter. Hints of grease lingered under Adam's nails. He looked dangerous and hot and Mel nearly swooned. "I can get off early on Wednesday and take Thursday off, if that works for you."

Mel nodded, showing him the map she'd printed. "That works. And I here's where I want to go."

He scrunched his nose. "Are you sure? The Wench can get kind of rough at night."

"I'm sure. And I've got personal time to use, so I'll take both days off. Maybe we can get a hotel and stay the night down there. That way we're not rushing back late. Separate rooms, of course."

He didn't respond at first, and she hazarded a look at him.

Adam stepped back and crossed his arms, his expression wary. "I don't know, Mel."

"We had an agreement, Adam. You promised to attract the kind of guy I want. Where do you suggest we do that around here? The frozen food aisle at the local grocery store? The Dirty Dog? You saw how well that went the other night." She matched his guarded body position, not giving an inch despite her nerves. "Like I said before, if you don't want to go with me, I'll find someone else. I can't quit now."

He took a deep breath, looking like he wanted to argue, but in the end all he did was shake his head. "You're not going there with Lilly. Two women alone at night isn't safe."

She gave him a flat stare. "Last time I checked you weren't my boss."

"You're right. I'm not. I'm your friend." His dark eyes turned stormy. "And I don't like the idea of you going to that place with Lilly or anyone else. Who knows what kind of trouble you'd get into."

Affront surged through her bloodstream. She might be a virgin, but that didn't make her an idiot. "For your information I graduated at the top of my self-defense class and have taken judo at the Y. I can take care of myself. And my trouble is none of your business. Especially if you break our agreement."

They glared at each other across the circulation desk as the air between them sizzled. Finally, Mel shrugged and turned away, her heart threatening to slam out of her ribcage. "Come or don't. Your choice."

One long beat stretched into two. Then three.

Please don't let him walk away. Please don't let him walk away.

Finally, Adam huffed out a breath behind her. "Fine. But we leave when I say, no arguments."

Mel managed not to fist pump, barely. To him, she said, "I don't need a babysitter."

"No, you need a mentor, a dating guru. That's what we agreed to. And if I'm doing the teaching, you listen to me. All right?"

She huffed out a breath. "Fine." It wasn't officially a date, but closer than Mel had gotten with him so far. She'd take it. "Pick me up at my house at four on Wednesday. That way we can get to Indy, check into our hotel and eat before we go out. I don't want to drink on an empty stomach. I'll make the reservations."

He nodded then left without another word, Mel watching him the whole way out.

ADAM TOOK another swig of dark lager as the classic cover band in the corner of the bar rocked out their version of "Enter Sandman" by Metallica.

He hadn't been to The Tipsy Wench since before he'd left for basic training a decade ago, but it didn't look like the place had changed much. Still a bit too rough and trashy for polite conversation—or conversation at all, really. A trendy dive-bar nightmare, filled by an odd mix of hipsters with man buns and tight jeans, rockers, and wannabe Goths with black clothes and eyeliner.

So. Much. Eyeliner.

Mel sat on a stool beside him at the bar, taking it all in like a kid on their first trip to Disneyland. She'd told Adam to stay out of sight in a corner, but he'd insisted on being where he could keep an eye on everything. Yes, he was here as her coach, but the idea of one of these guys groping her—or worse—made his head pound. He might not be an actual badass, but he could sure as hell fool these idiots into thinking he was. And if that kept some random dude from messing with Mel, so be it.

"What about him?" She pointed toward a guy across the room with hair a fauxhawk at least two feet high and a painful-looking piercing through his lip. "He seems interesting."

"Not him." Adam grimaced. "How would you kiss him around that thing in his mouth?"

"Good question." Mel frowned. "He's kind of cute, though. And I do like a bad boy."

Adam grunted, swallowing the words that teetered on the tip of his tongue. *Then you'll love me.*

Except he didn't want Mel loving him. Didn't want love at all.

Love only left you when you needed it most. Just like his mom had.

Better to keep emotions out of the equation when it came to relationships. What Mel needed was a nice, quiet, boring guy who'd keep her safe and secure. Like an insurance salesman or an accountant. Unfortunately, that type was nonexistent in this place.

He drained the rest of his lager in one long gulp then set the empty bottle on the bar. "Since there aren't any good prospects at the moment, how about a lesson instead?"

"What kind of lesson?"

"Small talk."

"Small talk?" Mel scrunched her nose.

"Yeah, you know, banter, flirting, verbal foreplay." He mentally punched himself for that last one as she blushed, and his body tightened against his will, but it was too late now. "You'll have to talk to your mystery man at some point, right? Unless you pay him."

"Okay. Go on. Teach me to flirt." Mel pressed closer to him and batted her eyelashes.

His pulse tripped. He straightened to increase the space between them and did his best to focus on the task at hand rather than the adorable woman beside him. "Uh, coming on too strong is not good. Now look at me like you're interested. Five-second rule."

She frowned. "The five-second rule?"

"When you find someone attractive at a party or whatever, hold their gaze for five seconds. If they come over, they're interested. If not, they aren't into you or they're taken."

Mel gave him a look that was more zombie than hot-chick-looking-for-a-mate.

"Relax." Adam gestured to the bartender for another lager for himself and refill on whatever frou-frou drink Mel had ordered. "Now smile. It makes you look more confident. Plus, you have a great grin. Brings out your dimples."

Mel's face lit up then, taking her from pretty to gorgeous. "You think I have a great grin? That's so sweet."

He frowned down at his toes as heat clawed up his cheeks. "C'mon. You know you're beautiful, so just stop."

"Ha! Got a compliment out of you!" She winked and Adam felt another one of the carefully constructed barriers around his heart begin to crumble. Before he could recover, she said, "Next flirting tip, please."

After clearing his throat, Adam continued, "Be who you are. Don't pretend to be something you're not to make people like you. The right person will love your intelligence and drive and strength, not be intimidated by them."

Mel gave him a pointed stare. "I never play dumb for anyone. I've got a mountain of student loan debt and a graduate degree to prove it."

He tipped his bottle to her. "Cheers. Next tip: when you find someone you think is right, don't be afraid to take charge.

Make it clear you're interested and get their number. If you say you're going to call, then call. And don't be afraid to touch their arm, put your hand on their shoulder, show affection, that sort of stuff."

Mel shifted then, running her foot up the side of Adam's shin, the caress freezing him in place, as his nervous system went haywire and his traitorous libido kicked into overdrive. She gave him an innocent look. "Like that?"

"Uh, yeah," he managed to mumble, his voice rougher than normal. "Maybe a little subtler though, especially at first."

This time she stroked his bare forearm, a light touch that had him stifling a tiny groan of pleasure. It had been so long since anyone had touched him like that—softly, tenderly, reverently. Then she broke the spell by turning away and sliding off her stool. "Great. Time to practice on someone else. What about him?"

Mel pointed to a new dude standing in the shadows with two other guys who were all dressed in ill-fitting suits, sporting ink on their hands and cheeks. Adam had seen the same designs on a couple of guys in his platoon. Prison tats. He'd bet money the trio had just come from court appearances. "Uh, *that* is a definite nope."

"Why?" Mel scowled, hands on hips. "They look like professionals."

Professional criminals, maybe. Adam snorted. "Not your type. Unless you like them from Cell Block C."

Mel gave him a peeved stare. "How do you know? You've seen them one time from across the room. You don't know anything about them."

"I know those suits probably came from the thrift shop,

based on the bad fit. I know the tats all three are sporting on their faces are symbols for how long their sentences were." He stood and fished his wallet out of his back pocket. "Come on. Let's get out of here."

"I'm not ready yet." Mel took another long sip of her drink. "I haven't met my quota."

"Quota?"

"I promised myself I'd talk to at least one new guy tonight." She patted her hair, which she'd worn up, with a few loose strands hanging down around her neck to give Adam all sorts of naughty ideas. As if riding here with her on his bike—her front pressed against his back, her hands clutching his waist—hadn't been bad enough. Like heaven and hell all rolled into one. The way her fingers gripped the front of his shirt as if she'd never let go. Adam leaned back against the bar. "Stop fussing. Your hair still looks perfect. The same as it did when we left the hotel earlier."

A server in the standard bar uniform of leather shorts and tight fuchsia tank top, strutted by, giving Adam a wink. The guy was more James's type than his, but Mel shot visual daggers at Adam anyway as he checked the crowd again for a suitable person for Mel to flirt with. "I don't think you're going to find what you're looking for in this place."

"How do you know? Maybe I'm in the mood for a quick booty call."

He busted out laughing. Couldn't help it. "Where'd you learn about booty calls?"

"I'm going to be twenty-five, Adam, not two hundred and five. And just because I've never had one doesn't mean I don't know what they are. I read *Cosmo*."

"I know. I saw the evidence on your coffee table the other night." He handed the bartender a fifty to cover a twelve-dollar tab. He could afford to be generous. They made good money at Victory Vets, and he saved most of his paychecks, other than for bills and home repairs. Adam couldn't resist a little flirting with her, even though it was tricky territory considering his reactions to her tonight. He watched Mel over the rim of his bottle, enjoying the way she flushed under his gaze. "Wow. I didn't realize you were a frisky girl at heart, Mel."

"I'm full of all sorts of surprises." She picked up her own glass and swirled the liquid inside. "Or maybe this place brings out my wild side." Then she smiled again, the one that went straight to his core. "Thank you, by the way. For being my wingman."

He blinked at her. "I'm your wingman?"

"You are."

As if drawn by some invisible cord, Adam found himself leaning closer to her, so close his breath stirred the wisps of hair at her temple. "Then as your wingman, I'm telling you that if you're so determined to flirt, let's try someplace else."

Her shoulders sagged slightly. "I think you're missing the potential—"

"There *is* no potential here." He straightened and took her hand. "C'mon. I know we've got a deadline on this project, but nobody here is even remotely good enough for you."

Me included.

Mel finished her drink as the cover band started a sappy rendition of "Sister Christian." She stopped, staring at the stage. "I love this song. How about one dance before we go. Please?"

He should have said no, should gone outside and gotten on his bike and headed for the safe, familiar confines of their separate hotel rooms. But instead, he let Mel lead him out onto the crowded dance floor. The space was small, and they had no choice but to press together to avoid bumping into anyone else. That's the excuse he was going with anyway.

As they swayed in time with music Adam did his best to remember why all of this was such a very bad idea. Then Mel slid her arms around his neck and twined her fingers into the hair at his nape, making Adam shudder against her. He gripped her waist, the material of her top silky beneath his fingertips. She chosen purple tonight, with a short black skirt.

All this was wrong, so wrong. And yet it felt so, so right.

Another couple brushed past them, and Adam pulled Mel even closer. She looked up at him, her eyes dreamy and soft, her full lips parted, and he couldn't look away, not if his life depended on it.

Time slowed as he bent and then his lips were on hers.

God help him, he'd wanted to kiss her again since that night in her foyer. One taste of Mel hadn't been enough, would never be enough. His heart pinched with yearning as he tightened his arms around her. Mel relaxed into him, lifting her chin and opening her mouth to give him better access.

He shouldn't be doing this. He didn't want to get involved with Mel. He didn't want to get close to anyone. He certainly didn't want to fall in love, but he couldn't seem to stop himself where Mel was concerned. Every look, every touch drew him further under her spell. She gave a little moan into his mouth, making him wonder when else she might make those kinds of noises...

Her little mewls of pleasure sent a fresh wave of desire through him, and he had to break away for fear of taking things too far, too fast. Breath ragged and hands shaking with need, Adam rested his forehead against hers. He had to stop. They had to stop. Because if he didn't Mel's first time would be right here in this seedy bar, and she was far too precious for that.

Adam licked his lips and tasted her there—sweet liquor and sinful desire. Mel tried to kiss him again, but he pulled back slightly. She looked as punch drunk of emotion as he felt. Her panting breaths only encouraged him to get the hell out of there before they couldn't anymore. Still, he couldn't resist running his thumb over her trembling bottom lip.

Big mistake. Her green eyes darkened, and her lashes fluttered as she nipped his thumb, and for a moment he forgot where he was, who he was and what he wasn't, forgot everything except her, in his arms.

Mine.

He'd never been an alpha sort of guy, but damn if Mel didn't bring out that side in him. He realized then that he didn't want her dating other men, test-driving them while he watched her, coached her. And he certainly didn't want her sleeping with anyone else. If she wanted to learn how to please a man, he'd do the job.

Still, he needed to be sure.

Adam gently tipped her face up to his until she met his gaze. "Mel, I want you. Is that what you want, too?"

In answer, her body melted into his and he cupped her butt, pulling her against the evidence of just how badly he wanted her. Mel grinned then, a wicked affair despite her innocence. "There's only ever been one man I wanted, but I didn't think you wanted me—"

He shook his head. "Believe me, Mel. Wanting you was never the problem."

She tilter her head, brows knitting. "Why now?"

"I don't know." The music ended, and the dance floor cleared. "I've either made up my mind or I've lost it completely."

Her seductive laugh coiled inside him, tightening the aching knot of need in his gut. She felt so warm and soft and perfect in his arms. He'd had well under his limit of lager tonight, but his inhibitions were suddenly gone. He pulled her in and kissed her once more—testing, tasting, teasing. She traced his jaw with one finger, a delicate touch that made him hurry outside to his bike, Mel in tow. He couldn't take much more of this exquisite torture. His body thrummed with anticipation, his blood sizzling through his veins.

Mel gazed at him with eyes full of promise. Never in his life had Adam wanted something as much as he wanted Mel tonight, and the thought both thrilled and terrified him.

She went on tiptoe and whispered in his ear, "Let's go back to the hotel."

CHAPTER NINE

Mel held tight to Adam as they zoomed through the midnight streets of downtown Indianapolis to their hotel at City Centre. She felt reckless and free and oddly apprehensive, now that the big moment was almost upon her. More than anything though, the thought of finally spending the night with the man of her dreams had her excited beyond all comprehension.

Anticipation, mixed with a good dose of nervous energy, had her heart racing and her nerve endings on high alert. Her hand clutched the soft shirt over his flat, toned abs, allowing her to feel his muscles flex each time the bike turned one way or another. He felt warm and strong and infinitely inviting. Her own skin felt too tight, and her blood sizzled through her veins. She'd waited twenty-four years for this night, and now her tension built higher, leaving her breathless for release. Given Adam's sharp intake of breath whenever she kissed the nape of his neck, he felt the same.

They pulled into the hotel's underground garage and parked in a spot near the elevators. Adam cut the engine and locked up the bike before pulling Mel into his arms, asking, "You're sure?"

"More than I've ever been about anything in my life."

They crashed into each other once more, a jumbled mass of arms, legs, and lips, her back pressed to the cold cement wall while they waited for the elevator to arrive. The bell dinged, and they tripped onboard, Adam blindly slapping the button for their floor while Mel gripped his rear, making them both laugh.

The ride upstairs was a blur. Somehow, they managed to exit the elevator while still kissing. In the hallway, Adam carried Mel down the hall toward their rooms, her legs wrapped around his waist. Then he pushed inside, giving them privacy at last. Mel got a brief view of polished wood floors and a bank of windows that glowed with the city's skyline, the same as her room, before Adam consumed all her attention again.

Need vibrated through her as they stood inches apart near the bed. Mel couldn't resist kissing his neck again, licking the salt from his throat as she'd fantasized doing so many times before. Then her tongue found the pulse point at the base of his neck, thudding hard, and she melted a little more at the knowledge that he was as affected by all this as she was.

Adam groaned low and pulled her closer to reclaim her lips.

"I want you so much," Mel whispered against his mouth, pulling away slightly to toy with the hem of his T-shirt. "I can't wait to make love with you."

His body tensed beneath her words, and Mel frowned. If he changed his mind now... No. She couldn't let that happen, not when she was so close to everything she'd ever wanted. She ran her hands down his back, kneading the bunched muscles between his shoulder blades, hoping to alleviate whatever was bothering him. When he still didn't relax, she pulled back, her heart sinking to her toes. "What's wrong?"

ADAM'S DESIRE for Mel threatened to burn him alive. There was nothing he wanted more than to tumble her down onto that bed and explore every luscious inch of her with his hands and lips and tongue, but he also knew that once they crossed this line, they could never go back. And her dropping the L-word just now, didn't help. "Nothing's wrong. I just..."

Mel took a deep breath, wincing slightly. "It's me, isn't it?"

"What? No!" He kissed the top of her head then resting his chin atop her hair. "No, Mel. It's not you. You're perfect. I just want to make sure we're still on the same page here..." He shook his head and stared across the room. "If we do this, it's just sex. You get that, right?"

Mel gave him a speculative look, her expression unread-able. Which was better than disappointment, he supposed. He'd disappointed far too many people he cared for in his life and he didn't want to add Mel to that list. That's why he needed to be brutally honest with her. He'd sleep with her, worship her glorious body from head to toe, still look out for her and keep her safe, but he couldn't love her. Couldn't love anybody. Not again.

Every fiber of his being yearned for the all-consuming fire

he felt with her, and he'd rather die than let her go, but he would, if that's what she wanted.

He feared that's exactly what would happen too, given she still hadn't said a word. Then she clutched the front of his shirt and yanked him closer, her serious gaze taking no prisoners. "We had an agreement, Adam. I don't go back on my word, and neither to you. Consider this another lesson. No emotions involved. That was our deal. Now, are you going to teach me a thing or two in this bed or what?"

Eyes wide, Adam blinked down at her, fresh adrenaline coursing through him, urging him onward. The spark of confidence in her eyes burned through his doubts. He couldn't resist a grin as his pulse galloped like a Thoroughbred stallion. He wasn't sure where this new, confident Mel had come from, but man, he liked her. "Probably more like seven or eight things at least, but we'll see how it goes."

Then they were all over each other again. His back hit the wall at the same moment her shirt came off. Adam reached behind her to unzip her skirt, his mouth drying as he watched it slid off her to land in a small puddle around her ankles. All that creamy, soft skin covered only by a few small scraps of lace was the most beautiful thing he'd ever seen. Her perfume—cherry blossoms and vanilla—intoxicated him far more than the alcohol at the bar ever would. He reached or her, but she stayed just out of his reach, keeping where he was with one finger pressed to the center of his chest.

"Strip." She'd gone from insecure to siren in two-seconds flat. "Now."

Adam obeyed, his eyes fixed to hers as he tugged his shirt

off over his head, tossing it aside before starting on his jeans. He made quick work of his fly as he toed off his boots, then stepped out of his pants, leaving him in just his boxer-briefs. Seeing Mel openly ogle him made Adam feel ten feet tall. And so hard he ached.

Unable to take any more, he kissed her, his lips skimming across her cheek and down her neck to the hollow at the base of her throat. He lavished attention there until she moaned, her head falling back. She was so responsive to his touch, a powerful aphrodisiac in itself. Her responses sent a delicious thrill through him, made him feel powerful, and more than a little possessive. Mel was his, at least for tonight, and he planned to take full advantage of that. He traced his tongue over her collarbone, loving her little gasp and how she thrust her fingers into his hair, her nails scraping his scalp as if she'd never let him go. It wasn't true, but a guy could pretend for a while.

Mel felt good. Tasted good. Smelled good. All his senses were in overdrive now, and he couldn't get enough. He picked her up, carrying her over to the windows, where he sat her on the marble ledge. She shuddered as her bare skin pressed against the cool glass, and he broke away to look into her passion-glazed eyes. This was her first time, and it had to be special.

No. Not just special. Perfect. If anyone deserved perfect, it was Mel, and even as broken and unworthy as Adam was, he vowed to give her that, if only this one time.

We had an agreement...No emotions involved...That was our deal.

Her earlier words haunted him before he shoved them

aside, his fingertips grazing her cheek, the simple touch sending another ripple of awareness through him. He wasn't sure how he'd let her go after all this was over, just that he would. But, for now, he wanted to relish every moment. He traced his knuckles down her chest to the valley between her breasts, smiling as her breath caught. "Years of fantasies are a lot to overcome. This should be a night to remember."

"I remember everything about you," Mel whispered.

His heart squeezed a little more. She was so sweet, so kind, so smart and innocent and good. Everything he wasn't. He'd had her on an untouchable pedestal for so long and now that she was here—ready and willing—and he wasn't sure how to handle it.

I remember everything about you.

There were times, growing up, he would've given anything in the world to hear someone say they treasured him enough to remember him. And Mel had handed him that gift with an open heart. He slid his hands down her back, settling them in the small curve above her rear as he pressed closer, allowing her to feel the full extent of his need for her. He couldn't give her his heart, but he could give her the rest of him, for what it was worth, for as long as they had together.

Adam picked her up again and walked backward toward the bed. The back of his legs hit the mattress, and he stopped, turning to place Mel on the bed first before stretching out beside her, his body trembling with barely leashed need.

"You're sure about this?" he asked one last time, needing reassurance that all this was real and he wasn't just imagining it all.

"Yes." She traced her fingers down his chest to the waistband of his underwear. "Beyond sure."

Adam trailed kisses from her lips to her ear, then down the side of her neck. She arched against him, her breath panting hot against his skin, doing his best to maintain control as he forced words past his tight vocal cords. "Slow and easy."

"Or fast and furious." Mel pulled away slightly, her cheeks flushed and eyes dark with passion. Then her little grin turned positively wicked as she tugged him close once more. "It's a woman's prerogative to change her mind, right?"

THE NEXT MORNING, Mel blinked her eyes open as first rays of sunshine peeked through the windows. They'd fallen asleep in each other's arms, and she had no idea how long they'd slept. It was Saturday, and she had the rare weekend off, so it didn't matter. She had nowhere to be today. Nowhere except here, with Adam, her lover.

Lover.

A shiver ran through her as memories of their night together resurfaced. The wicked things he'd done to her last night, the wicked things she'd done to him. All the wicked things they'd done together. Being with him had been incredible, unforgettable, unbelievably erotic, and yet so sweet her chest still ached from it.

Adam snored softly beside her, his face turned away, one arm hugging the pillow beneath his head. She snuggled in behind him, her chin resting on his shoulder as she traced a finger over the dark stubble now covering his jaw. She kissed his nape, inhaling his scent, so familiar now. Then she counted the freckles on his upper back, stopping to kiss each one. He'd been sweet and tender with her, but also demanding, not letting her hide from her passion for one second, drawing every ounce of sensation from her before taking his own release. Her body ached this morning, a new pleasant sensation she wasn't sure she'd ever forget. She'd lost her virginity last night. With Adam Foster. She flopped onto her back, stifling a squeal of delight. Who would have ever guessed?

Her restless movements must've awakened Adam, because next thing she knew, he rolled over to face her, yawning, then kissing her temple. "'Morning," he said, his voice groggy and gruff. Then he propped up on one elbow and smiled wide at her. "You're amazing."

Mel giggled, burying her heated face in the covers, suddenly shy. "You're not so bad yourself."

Adam chuckled, reaching over to uncover her eyes, giving her an amused look. "Seriously though, are you okay this morning?" He shifted lower so their faces aligned. "Need anything? Water? Food? Ibuprofen? I always keep a bottle handy in my duffel bag."

"I'm good." Mel meant it. And even if she wasn't, the last thing she wanted was for Adam to get up and leave the bed. She wanted him staying right where he was. "Never better."

He kissed her then, soft and tender, before leaning back to study her, while a million questions swirled through Mel's mind. Had she done all the right things last night? Had she pleased him as much as he'd pleasured her? Had it been good for him too?

Each time she closed her eyes, she remembered being in his

arms, the way he'd moved and tasted and sounded, his dark gaze locked on her, hot with desire. Seducing her bad boy had been all she'd ever dreamed of and more, and she couldn't wait to do it again.

We had an agreement...No emotions involved...That was our deal.

Her heart gave a painful pinch as she recalled her words to him last night. She shouldn't have brought up their agreement, but she'd been so afraid he was going to back out after her stupid remark about making love. She'd known what she was getting into with him from the start. Adam didn't do love. He'd been honest with her about that, and she'd agreed to accept him as he was. Still, she couldn't squelch her bit of disappointment that maybe he'd changed, that maybe *she'd* changed his mind.

Mel shook off those silly thoughts though. That was her old self talking. The new her lived for the moment, threw caution to the wind, took life as it came. No rules. No expectations.

She turned on her side to find Adam snoozing once more beside her, one arm thrown over his eyes, his breath even and deep. Mel couldn't resist running her fingers down his torso, over the smattering of dark hair covering his pecs narrowing to a line bisecting his taut abs, then disappearing beneath the covers, which were gathered low on his hips. Mel licked her lips as her hand disappeared beneath the sheet.

"Whoa there cowgirl." Adam lifted his arm, peeking at her with one eye as his other hand caught hers. He gave her a brazen once-over, his sleepy dark eyes sparkling with mischief. "Are you sure you're ready for another round?"

"This ain't my first rodeo." Mel waggled her brows at him, laughing at the truth of it now as he tumbled her over onto her back, his arms around her and his mouth claiming hers. Processing all her jumbled emotions over this could happen later. Given her birthday was only a few short weeks away, reality would return soon enough. Today though, she'd treasure what she had, right here in the present.

CHAPTER TEN

Mel felt like she had the words "wanton woman" stamped across her forehead as she sat at her parents' dining room table that Sunday, sans Adam. He'd left her house earlier in the day, telling her it was probably best for them to not be seen together so soon after doing the deed. Given how her skin felt imprinted with his every touch and kiss, that was probably true.

Besides, today was weird enough as it was. Sunday dinners at the Bryant house were never this... *quiet.*

Something was definitely up.

Finally, her mother broke the tension. "We have a surprise. James is coming home a day early! August thirteenth. So he'll be here for your birthday."

It took Mel's sex-drugged brain a second to process that. Then she frowned. Keeping what she and Adam were doing a secret would be harder with her brother around. This wasn't exactly wonderful news. Still, she forced a smile. "Great."

"He's looking forward to getting home and settling in here again," her dad added. "Be great to have him around again, huh?"

"Yeah." Mel slumped back in her seat. She was happy James would be home again, safe and sound, but things had just taken an interesting turn between her and Adam. She wasn't ready for that to end yet. She rubbed her forehead, feeling the weight of her mother's stare watching her curiously. "What time is he arriving?"

"You can ask him yourself," her mother said, pointing to her cell phone on the table. "He's due to call any minute."

She really didn't want to talk to her brother without going over it with Adam first, so Mel stood and picked up her half-finished plate, heading for the kitchen.

"Aren't you going to eat more, honey?" her mother called after her.

"I'm not very hungry," Mel called back.

The phone rang as she was rinsing off her plate to put it in the dishwasher. Through the open doorway, her parents' cheerful voices echoed. Mel cringed. She had to talk to Adam, sooner rather than later, even though part of her wished they could stay in their blissful bubble of solitude from the hotel and not deal with the outside world or their agreement just yet.

She'd just finished drying her hands when her mother walked into the kitchen and handed the phone to Mel. "James wants to say hi."

Mel took it reluctantly, ducking out the back door into the yard where she could have a little privacy, heading to a stone bench set amongst the flowering hedges. Forcing a cheerfulness she didn't feel, Mel greeted her brother. "Hey, James. Congratulations on coming home early."

"Thanks," he said. "Can't wait to see everyone again. Is everything okay there?"

"Sure," she said, too fast, then winced. "Things are great here."

Or they had been, yesterday, in bed with Adam.

Not that she'd ever tell her brother about that.

A beat or two passed before James asked, "What's wrong?"

Uh-oh. He'd always been far too good at reading people, a skill he'd said came from being queer and needing to know who was safe and who wasn't.

"Nothing's wrong. I'm just tired," she said, hoping the lie sounded more convincing than it felt. "How are things with you?"

"They'll be better once I get out of this desert. Have you seen Adam?"

"Uh..." Her throat dried and her heart tumbled to her toes. She hated lying to her brother, but then what she expected when she made that deal with his best friend? "No. Why?"

"No reason," James said, his tone regular and even. "I talked to the guys from Victory Vets earlier and one of them said they thought they saw you two hanging out together recently."

"Oh, um..." She scrambled for a plausible reason for her to spend time with Adam that wouldn't send up all sorts of red flags. "I had some issues with my car, and he was taking a look at it for me."

Part of her wanted to tell James to just mind his own business, along with all his buddies at the garage, but in a town the size of Point Beacon that wasn't really feasible. Gossip was basically the town's number one export.

"I mean, I don't care what you two do," James said, and the swell of love inside her for him brought tears to her eyes. If anyone knew the meaning of discretion, it was a gay man. "But it would be nice to know, sis. I mean, I've told you all my secrets."

True. Which only made her feel more guilty. But she wasn't the only one in the equation here and she really needed to talk to Adam first before she said anything to anyone. With everything that had happened that weekend, her emotions were still in a jumble.

"Okay, well if you're not going to spill the tea, then I'm going to go. I've been trying to call Adam, but just get his voicemail. Do you know where he is?"

"Nope." The truth, for once. Honestly, she'd tried calling him earlier too, but had ended up leaving a message.

"Right." James said something to someone offline, then to Mel. "Okay, well I'm going then. Stay safe, sis. Since your new makeover I hear you're a hot ticket around town. I don't want you to get hurt."

"I'm fine, don't worry," she said, glancing over at the house to see her parents watching her through the window over the kitchen sink. "See you soon, James. Love you."

"Love you too, sis," he said before ending the call.

Mel went back inside, handing the phone to her father before kissing both her parents on the cheek and heading home. It was a nice day out, so she'd walked there and hoped the exercise would do her good; clear her head a bit.

She shouldn't feel guilty about not telling James about her

and Adam because it wasn't really a relationship anyway. In fact, they'd gone out of their way to make sure they both knew it *wasn't* a relationship. Their arrangement was temporary and would be over anyway in a few weeks when her birthday hit. So she'd done nothing wrong on that phone call.

Still, she thought she should feel better about it than she did.

Sunshine prickled her skin with warmth as a steady breeze cooled her heated cheeks. The smell of freshly mown grass filled the air and the sounds of kids playing basketball drifted from the park nearby.

Her parents were throwing a party for Mel, as they did every year for each kid's birthday, and this year they'd probably add in a hearty welcome for James too. That was good.

But how would she deal with Adam being there, with this deal between them finally coming to an end. Being with him had been...amazing. Beyond amazing. And if she was honest with herself, she'd love to keep that going, at least for a little longer.

Originally, she'd been terrified of dying a dried-up old spinster. But now that she'd been with Adam, experienced how wonderful intimacy could be with the right person, she feared never having that again after him. Chemistry like theirs had to be rare, right?

She had two weeks left until James came home. Two weeks until reality returned and she needed to figure all this out. Two weeks to talk to Adam and find out how he wanted to handle things.

He didn't do love, but maybe he did do "friends with benefits?"

The question was, could she?

ON MONDAY ADAM watched the clock. Which was weird because he'd never had a problem keeping his mind on the job before.

But now his thoughts were filled with Mel. Waking up next to her, talking to her, making love to her. Because yeah, regardless of his denials, what they'd done had gone far beyond just sex. At least for him.

He wasn't sure how he felt about that. All he knew was that he'd struggled all morning to suppress the grin that kept wanting to show on his face.

He'd gone over to her place last night to hang out, lying around in her living room, reading that *Cosmo* sex book of hers together, then trying some of the "variations" in bed.

Being with her was different than anything he'd ever experienced before. She was so open and trusting with him, and her eagerness and playfulness and responsiveness during sex.... His Mel was a natural in the sack. Hell, she'd even taught a jaded player like him a few new tricks.

His mind stopped short.

My Mel?

He sobered and began tinkering with the engine he was rebuilding again. He wasn't sure where that had come from, just that it needed to go away. Fast. He didn't love Mel. He didn't *do* love, period. They had a deal, an agreement. No way would he mess that up now.

It was just that he liked her, he told himself. A lot. More

than he'd expected. They'd been friends in high school, sure, but now they were both grown up and had lived more life. And he liked her even better now because of it.

But love? Nope. He'd locked all those emotions away a long time ago, the day his mother had walked out on him and his dad, and they'd been buried so deep he doubted they were even alive anymore.

Adam frowned down at the Hemi V8. God, what was happening to him? A couple great nights between the sheets and he was losing it.

Besides, Mel wasn't his type anyway. She was way too good for the likes of him. She needed a man who could provide her with the kind of life she deserved; a man who would take care of her and give her his whole heart. Adam didn't know if the scarred remnants he had could even be called a heart. In the past, it hadn't bothered him, knowing that he'd be alone for the rest of his life. But now, since being with Mel, for some reason he'd begun feeling this weird ache in his chest whenever he imagined his vast future by himself.

A more emotional man might have called it loneliness.

Good thing Adam didn't put much stock in his feelings.

No, best to stick with things as they were. Mel had never mentioned changing their deal or taking things between them to the next level, and he wouldn't either. He'd agreed to help her find a guy, someone she could date and possibly marry one day. That wasn't him. Never would be. Not after the disaster he'd witnessed between his own parents.

But the Bryants were different. They supported each other, loved each other, enjoyed spending time with each other.

He rubbed the sore spot over his heart, then set his tools aside, his fingers coated in thick black grease.

There'd been several missed calls from his buddy James on his phone from yesterday too, and this morning, but he hadn't called him back yet. Figured he'd do that later after he talked to Mel, in case there was something he needed to know first.

The phone at Victory Vets rang and Miguel answered, then began typing on the computer, probably setting up an appointment for a customer.

With a sigh, Adam looked at the clock again, counting down the minutes to lunch. Mel had left him with a kiss that morning, asking Adam to meet her at the new sushi place on the town square as he'd walked out her door. They'd yet to spend the night at his place, which was just what Adam wanted. His house was a pit compared to her place, and he didn't want her to be uncomfortable there. That's what he told himself anyway. The fact he'd be embarrassed for her to see it lurked beneath it all too though.

Finally, after another hour of work on the engine, Miguel walked over and slapped Adam on the back. "Time for a lunch, dude."

Adam went to the restroom and scrubbed up as best he could in the sink, before staring at his reflection in the mirror. He'd drive himself nuts if he kept in his own head much longer. He needed to get out and get some fresh air and, most importantly, see Mel again.

After grabbing his wallet from the office safe, he walked down the block toward the restaurant where he was meeting Mel. She was waiting for him outside when he arrived, and without thinking, he leaned in for a kiss, only to have her pull away fast.

"Not here," she whispered, looking around to make sure no one had seen them. "We're still on the down-low, right?"

Gut tight, Adam grumbled as he opened the door for her, "Right."

Every eye in Fukiyama's seemed to turn in their direction as they entered. Or maybe that was just Adam's imagination since he seemed hyperaware of everything when Mel was around. The place was decorated nicely enough, with white linen tablecloths and fake Asian artwork on the walls. Looked popular too, with about three-quarters of the seats filled. An assortment of Point Beacon's elite were there—the mayor and his wife, the high school principal and her assistant, the bank manager.

Adam began sweating a little and resisted the urge to run his finger under the collar of his black shirt. He didn't belong here, not really, but it was where Mel wanted to eat and it made her happy, so he'd do it. Several police officers sat at a booth in the corner. He recognized them from run-ins they'd had with his father at one time or another over the years.

You're a respected business owner now.

Finally, a hostess led them to a table near the back. Adam kept his head down and his mouth shut as they took their seats. He'd learned a long time ago that keeping your mouth shut and your profile low saved you a lot of trouble in the end.

A server came and took their orders, then Adam sat back, allowing some of the tension in his shoulders to relax at last. He should enjoy this time together. They were getting near the end of their agreement, then he wouldn't have lunches with Mel anymore.

The ache in his chest intensified.

To cover it, Adam flashed Mel his most charming smile, as the server returned with their drinks—iced tea for her and a soda for him.

Mel smiled back, and Adam's whole world brightened.

He might not have any clue what he was really doing here and there might be hell to pay later for it later, but right now he couldn't bring himself to care. All that mattered was the fact that she'd filled a hole in his life he hadn't even known was there, and he'd sacrifice everything he had, everything he was, to have that for a little longer.

CHAPTER ELEVEN

"I'm stuffed." Mel pushed her plate away and sat back after lunch. "Ugh, I'll be lucky not to end up face-down in the stacks this afternoon for a nap. And now that you know I'm a sushi addict, please remind me not to overindulge next time?"

She stopped, hesitating as she realized what she'd assumed. That there *would* be a next time.

Thankfully, Adam didn't seem to notice, apparently fascinated with whatever was happening out the window behind Mel. Unsure what was wrong, but sure something had changed, she asked him, "Everything okay?"

"What?" He looked back at her, clearly distracted as he checked his watch. "Sorry. I need to get back to Victory Vets. Full schedule this afternoon."

"Oh. Sure." Confused and concerned that she'd done something wrong, Mel detangled her feet from his beneath the table and as she scooted out of the booth. Despite sleeping together, this was all new for her, and she was still learning how to do the whole relationship thing. *Except this isn't a relationship,* she reminded herself. "We should get back. Lunchtime's nearly over for me too."

Adam paid the bill at the register, despite Mel's insistence they split it, then they walked back outside to a tourist season in full swing. Even here in tiny Point Beacon, the local festivals brought in people from far and wide. Mel started back toward the library, only to have Adam take her arm and steer her around the corner of the building into a cool, deserted alley, giving them a bit of privacy.

She thought maybe he wanted to steal a quick kiss, only to be disappointed when Adam gave her a quizzical look instead. "This is all still pretend, right?"

"Uh..." Caught off guard, Mel wasn't sure what to say. Part of her had wished this could be a real date between them, but that was against their agreement. She had to stick to their deal or risk scaring him off completely. "Uh... sure."

Liar. Mel could tell herself she was able to keep her emotions out of this whole thing until the cows came home, but where Adam was concerned, but it wasn't true. Had never been true, honestly. She'd set out to seduce him, and she had, but that only led her to wanting more from him.

More he'd explicitly said he wouldn't give her in return.

Couldn't give her.

Her stomach tightened in a way that had nothing to do with all the sushi she'd just eaten.

Adam gave her a dubious look. "Because we had a deal."

"I know we had a deal, Adam," she snapped, suddenly irritated. With him or herself, she wasn't sure. "I'm not an idiot."

That's up for debate, seeing as how you've fallen for him.

No. No, no, no.

That wasn't true. She didn't love Adam Foster. That was nuts. She liked him, always had. He was nice and funny and sweet and sexy. And sure, she enjoyed spending time with him, sleeping with him, cuddling with him afterward. That wasn't love. Couldn't be love.

"We're still open to dating other people," he said. Not a question.

"Of course," she said, sidling around him to walk toward the sidewalk again. "Why you find a new bed partner already?"

"No." He scowled, following after her. For a brief moment she saw a flicker of pain in his dark eyes, there then gone, so fast she might've imagined it. "I just wanted to make sure we were still on the same page."

"Yep." Mel smoothed a hand down the front of her snazzy pink-and-white sheath dress with the shorter skirt and the boat-neck top she'd bought during their shopping excursion to the mall in Indy. That day seemed like forever ago now even though it was just a couple of weeks. Before this whole makeover with Adam, she never would've worn such bold colors or body-conscious styles, at least not without a baggy cardigan atop it, but then she was a different person now, wasn't she? Yes, she was. She forced a confident smile she didn't quite feel as they walked out onto the busy sidewalk again. "That's what we agreed to, right?"

"Right." He exhaled slowly, sliding on his sunglasses. "I'll meet you at Clem's after work. But I don't want to be out late. Okay?"

Nodding, Mel blinked hard at the ridiculous sting in her eyes. They'd planned to continue her flirting training tonight, even though flirting with other men was the last thing she wanted to do at present. Still, Adam had agreed to help her with her search for a guy, and he'd keep his word because he was steadfast. It was one of the things she loved most about him.

Not yours to love, she reminded herself. "Okay."

Distance. That's what she needed. To put some space between herself and this man who so easily evoked her deepest emotions without even trying. He had her so torn and twisted now she didn't know if she was coming or going.

"Hey, y'all," Lilly called, crossing the street to join them. Adam took another step away from Mel's side, and she missed his warmth immediately.

Lilly gave them a curious stare. "Am I interrupting something?"

"Not at all," Mel said, keeping her tone light. "We both happened to be eating lunch at the sushi place, so we shared a table because it was busy. Why?"

"No reason." Lilly glanced at Adam. "I need to steal Mr. Fixit here, if you don't mind. Car issues."

"I'm on my way back to the garage now." Adam stopped. "Why don't you just meet me there and I'll take a look."

"Sounds good," Lilly said, waving as Adam walked away.

Mel stared after him for a moment before returning her attention to her best friend. "Car issues?"

"I need an oil change," Lilly said, keeping pace with Mel's brisk steps as they neared the library. "James called me last night."

"Oh yeah?" Mel said, as they stopped at a small courtyard outside the library and took a seat on a wrought iron bench the local Lions club had installed the year before in honor of Point Beacon's fallen veterans and first responders. Mel was late already getting back but being figured being head librarian had to have some perks. "What did he want?"

"He said he got an email from the mayor about helping to chair the fall festival this year. Since I'm doing the official photography again, he had some questions about what was involved."

"Cool." Mel honestly couldn't care less what her brother did when he got back to town, but figured heading the festival might keep him busy and out of her hair where Adam and their deal was concerned, which was good. She looked up and found her best friend watching her closely. "What?"

"Is anything going on with you and Adam Foster?" Lilly asked, and Mel's heart tumbled to her toes. *Am I that obvious?*

"No. We had lunch, that's all." *And spent the night together in Indy where he rocked my universe.* No way was she sharing *that* with her best friend. Not now. Maybe not ever, depending on how things turned out. "Why do you care?"

Lilly shrugged, staring out across the courtyard. "Adam's a great guy, but he's not forever, that's all. I'd just hate to see you get hurt because of this crazy idea you have about finding a guy by your birthday. You deserve it all, Mel."

And there it was again. Everyone treating Mel like some delicate porcelain that would break with the slightest touch. She appreciated her friend's care, but she was tired of living under the weight of everyone else's expectations. "Nothing's going on between us Lils. And even if it was, I can take care of myself."

"Can you?" She met Mel's eyes, then looked away again.

"I'm sorry. It's none of my business. You're right. Just be careful with him, okay? Once a player always a player. I'm sorry to say that about Adam, but it's true. He's not looking to settle down and never will be."

Mel's hackles rose as she crossed her arms. "Maybe I'm just looking for a little fun too. And if I wanted to sleep with a player like Adam Foster, that's my choice. Maybe I'm a player too."

Lilly snorted. "Right."

Embarrassed and hurt, Mel pushed to her feet and started to walk away, only to have her best friend grab her arm.

"Wait. I'm sorry, Mel," she said. "You wanted to make changes. I get that. I do. But thinking things with Adam will go any farther than a fling is setting yourself up for disaster. I know you, Mel. You couldn't keep your heart out of the equation if you tried. You're all heart. That's why I love you. So, please, just be careful with him, okay?"

Mel pulled free with a mirthless laugh. "God, why is everyone so concerned about me? Believe me, I'm well aware of Adam's reputation. I spent too many years tagging along after him and my brother not to know what he's really like. But people change, Lilly."

"Do they?" Lilly asked, standing herself. "Take care, Mel."

As she watched her best friend walk away, Mel couldn't help replaying Adam's words from earlier in her head.

We're still open to dating other people...

Was that Adam's way of telling her he wanted out of their deal?

Maybe, she supposed, but she wasn't ready to give up on this thing between them yet either way. She'd been crushing on him for over a decade. He ticked all the boxes on her wish list and more. But Mel wasn't stupid. And she wasn't naive, either, despite what Lilly and everyone else apparently thought. She'd handle this thing with Adam until their deal was done and then she'd let him go.

Because that's what she'd agreed to do.

And if he wanted to see other people in the meantime, well, she had no right to tell him not to. She could see other people too. In fact, maybe she'd meet someone new at Clem's tonight and all this angst would be over.

Mel turned toward the library doors, savoring a few more precious seconds of summer sun. People milled past, some she recognized as locals, some she pegged as tourists, all of them going about their business without a care.

She was determined to do the same as she walked back into the library and headed for the circulation desk.

THE LONGER ADAM sat in Clem's that night, watching Mel play pool with some random dude, the more he regretted his decision to come tonight. They'd only been there forty-five minutes, and it already felt like forever.

He clenched his beer bottle tighter as the guy made his moves on Mel, and she gave the dude a coy smile with a sparkle in her eyes. He knew that sparkle, dammit, and something in Adam's chest tightened uncomfortably.

She was learning how to flirt fast.

Too fast.

Of course, the fact she was wearing new jeans that cupped

her butt to perfection and made Adam want to pull her onto his lap and keep her there didn't help either.

From the minute he'd picked her up at her house after work, and he couldn't stop himself from watching the sway of her hips as she'd walked in front of him to his bike, he'd known he was in trouble.

She'd insisted on trying things by herself tonight at the bar, with him there only if needed, so he'd plopped himself down on a stool and down his best to watch the game on the TV in the corner and not how Mel had proceeded to charm all the single men in the room.

He sighed and took the last swig from his bottle, wishing he'd ordered something stronger. *What the hell is wrong with me?* Mel was doing exactly what he'd wanted her to do, what *she'd* said she wanted to do—learning how to date. But now that their project was a success, Adam thought he'd feel a lot better about it than he did.

In fact, every time a new man joined the group of guys drawn to Mel like bugs to a zapper, he wanted to punch his fist though the nearest wall, which wasn't like him at all.

Then Mel's husky laugh drifted through the air toward him, its sensual tone rivaling the country tunes streaming from the old jukebox against the wall. His muscles tightened, and sweat prickled his skin, and he had images of himself stalking over to that pool table and tossing Mel over his shoulder before hauling her out of there, caveman style.

If he didn't know better, he'd think he was jealous.

Except being jealous involved love, and Adam didn't do that.

No. He wasn't jealous. He just didn't like the way Mr.

Handsy over there had put his arm around Mel's waist as he'd pulled out his cell phone to punch in her digits. And he really disliked how every single man in the room was staring at her now as she crossed the room toward Adam.

He flagged down the waiter and ordered another beer as she slid onto her stool beside him with a satisfied smile.

"That was fun," Mel said. "That one guy even asked me for my number? *That* never happens. Usually they can't get away from me fast enough."

Adam grunted and kept his eyes on the TV screen. He couldn't name which teams were playing if his life depended on it, but it was better than grabbing Mel and kissing her until they both forgot all about their stupid deal.

He was overreacting, probably because it had been a busy day at the garage, and he needed time to unwind. That was all. Mel could do as she pleased in here, with whomever she please. She didn't belong to him. And they certainly weren't a couple.

That's why he'd asked about dating other people earlier at lunch. To make sure they were both still on the same page here. He was only here to help. Her hard work was finally paying off, and he had no business being pissy about it now.

And sure, they had sex. Good sex. Great sex. But that didn't mean it came with any strings or deeper emotions attached. It was another lesson for her, that was all.

He swiped the back of his hand over his sweaty forehead, wondering when it had gotten so hot in there.

Onscreen, the announcers were discussing the game during halftime. This used to be the time when his dad would get up and get more booze. If he was still awake. Sometimes he'd pass out before then.

Sometimes he wouldn't, and if his team lost, then he'd take his anger and disappointment out on Adam and his mom before she left. Afterward, it was just Adam, taking it on his own.

He shuddered at looked down at his beer instead. Watching the game hadn't been a good idea after all. It reminded him of all the reasons why he never should have agreed to help Mel at all. He didn't do love. He didn't know the first thing about long-term, healthy relationships. He was just some kid from the wrong side of the tracks, not worthy to pick up her trash, let alone touch her, hold her...

He shook off the errant thoughts and took another swig of beer.

"Can I tell you a secret?" Mel asked him, leaning in so her sweet cherry scent tickled his nose. "The number I gave that guy was made up." She giggled. "He's just not my type. Too buttoned-up and bossy."

For some stupid reason, that made happiness burst inside Adam like fireworks. He shrugged, shoving that ill-placed joy aside as he dug out his wallet and tossed a couple of bills on the bar to cover his tab. "He'll live. I need some food. Let's go grab a burger."

Mel took her purse and followed him toward the door. As they walked down the street toward a little dive diner called Boxer's, a place with a 1930s kitsch vibe and silver steel walls, Adam did his best to keep his hands to himself and his gaze straight ahead. Her birthday was drawing closer, and soon this would all be over. He could get through this. He would get through this. Then he'd go back to his happy single life and get on with it.

The thought of being alone again left him oddly empty.

He'd never had a problem staying on his own before. In fact, he preferred it. Things were safer that way. No one to impress. No one to worry about. No one to disappoint.

In the distance, a lonely train whistle blew, and the warm night breeze carried the sound of crops rustling and the smell of fresh growing things. If he'd been a hopeful man, Adam might have thought it was a sign of new beginnings. Too bad he wasn't.

They rounded a corner, and Mel smiled wide, seemingly oblivious to his sour mood. "I love Boxers! Best burgers in Indiana."

They walked inside and grabbed the last booth farthest from the door, Mel greeting people on the way while Adam kept his head down. Mel continued to chatter, her tone bright as they settled in their seats. "We used to have a place like this not far from the dorms when I was in college," she said, grabbing a menu from the holder. "Not nearly as good as this though. More like a greasy spoon. But man, the all-nighters we spent there, cramming for finals."

Adam hazarded a glance at her over the top of his own menu then. "You pulled all-nighters to study?"

"Sure." Mel gave a sad little chuckle. "I wanted to be the best in class, so I had to. It also helped that I had no social life. I was in bed by ten every night, never went to the bars. No frat parties, either. I wasn't invited to those." She studied the little daily specials card from the condiment holder. "Doesn't matter now, I guess."

His heart ached at her wistful tone and made him change the subject. "What are you having?"

In the end, they both ended up with the same thing—cheeseburgers, fries, and chocolate malts.

He'd figured bringing Mel here was a safe choice after the bar, but man. If he'd thought seeing her in those jeans had him worked up, then watching her eat a hamburger was nearly pornographic. She groaned with pleasure after every bite, and the way she licked the ketchup from her fingers should carry an indecency charge in all fifty states. But the worst was how her head fell back and her eyes slid closed in pleasure when she sipped her malt, almost exactly the same way they had when she'd climaxed in Adam's arms. And now he was shifting in his seat to avoid an embarrassing situation down below.

"Can I get you two anything else right now?" the server asked as she stopped by their table, eliciting an irritated growl from Adam.

Mel shot him a confused glance at his odd reaction then smiled at the server. "I think we're good, thanks. And I'll take the check, please."

Adam took a big gulp of ice water hoping to cool his over-heated libido, scowling at Mel. "I've got this."

"No. You paid for lunch earlier." Mel slapped his hand away when the server returned with their bill. "I'm paying tonight. Partners, remember?"

"C'mon, Mel. I invited you here." He tried again to grab the paper slip and failed.

"Stop." She pulled a card from her wallet and handed it to the server as they passed by the table again. "There. Done."

Adam exhaled, his shoulders slumping slightly. He might not be a decent date in any other way, but the man should pay.

That was how he'd been raised by his momma. And, well, he wasn't used to other people doing things for him.

In fact, this whole thing with Mel had been as much of a learning experience for him as it was for Mel, and it left him discombobulated. He didn't know if he was up or down these days. All he knew was that whatever emotions were roiling around inside of him now because of her, they were not—would never be—love.

Love was a four-letter-word where he was concerned. Everything he'd ever seen of it, apart from the Bryants' home, was pain and loss and devastation. He refused to risk the life he'd worked so hard to build for himself after returning home on that.

Adam's palms itched and his skin felt too tight for his body. He'd gone into this to help Mel find her mojo, but he'd apparently lost his own because he had no clue what he was doing now.

He wiped his damp palms on his jeans, his stomach knotting the same way it had the day he'd walked to school after his mom left them, wearing the same clothes as the day before because there weren't any clean ones. His dad didn't do laundry and Adam hadn't had a clue then. He should end this now. Tell Mel he was sorry, but she'd have to find a guy on her own now. He'd given her the tools she needed, now it was up to her to use them.

Instead, when he opened his mouth, what came out was, "Miguel at the shop is getting married next weekend in Chicago. Want to go with me?"

Idiot.

As if things weren't confusing enough for him now. Add a couple days away in a hotel to the mix, dumbass.

Mel blinked at him, seemingly as surprised by the question as he was. "Oh, uh... I'll have to check my schedule at work." She frowned. "Won't the other guys from the garage be there too? I thought we were keeping this thing with us secret."

We are. "I'll tell everyone we're just friends and you're attending on James's behalf since can't be there."

Or you could have just not gotten yourself in this mess to begin with.

But now that the question was out there, he couldn't seem to make himself retract it. In fact, he couldn't think of anyone he'd rather sit through the long, boring Catholic ceremony with besides Mel.

She seemed to consider that a moment, stirring the last of her malt around in her glass before drinking it. "Well, I suppose that might work. I haven't been to Chicago in ages. I'll still have to check my schedule at the library and let you know for sure, but okay."

He flushed with joy at her answer even though he knew it was a horrible idea. No way was he going to get out of this unscathed, one way or another. "I'm thinking we drive up Friday night and spend the night so we don't have to rush around on Saturday before the wedding. Then we can come home on Sunday." He swallowed hard against the sudden lump in his throat, not wanting to assume anything, his pulse thumping hard behind his temples. "I already have a room reserved. We can share it, or I can call and—"

He hadn't realized until then just how badly he wanted her to say with him.

Mel gave him a look, then chuckled. "Let's just use your room. Unless you have a problem with that?"

He shook his head and released the breath he'd been holding. "Sounds good."

Man, he had it bad here and that wasn't good.

"Great." Mel smiled at him again, brightening his whole night. "I'll have to go shopping again, to buy something to wear, but I can to that online now that I know what works for me."

"Awesome," Adam said, sounding the opposite. He'd been the one to ask her to go but now he felt like an animal in a trap. *So stupid.* He tried to lighten his mood by adding, "They're doing a traditional Mexican reception."

"Oh, that sounds so cool!" Mel practically glowed with excitement now, and Adam's poor battered heart came alive. How was she so beautiful, and he'd never noticed before? No. That wasn't true. He'd always noticed Mel. She was so sweet and kind and generous with her time and attention and affection. How could he not notice her? But, before, he'd always held back, kept his barriers high and tight against her. Since that night in Indy though, all bets were off.

"Hey?" She reached across to tap his hand. "You okay?"

"Fine." He shrugged, not looking at her, afraid of what she'd see on his face. "Long day."

"Did you get Lilly's car fixed?" she asked, thankfully changing the subject.

"I did." He rolled his tense shoulder. "Faulty starter."

"I hate it when that happens," Mel said, her tone a bit naughty, and damn if Adam didn't feel it all the way to his groin. Their gazes locked again as she scooted out of her side of the booth, and he followed, trailing her out of the diner, feeling like a man walking the green mile, but he couldn't bring himself to stop. Not yet.

Outside, in the darkness, she entwined her fingers with his and Adam felt himself felt his heart crack a little more.

"I'm excited about this weekend." She rested her head against his arm as they strolled toward his bike still parked near Clem's. "Thanks for asking me."

He couldn't very well tell her it was a mistake, not now, not with her cuddled into his side, all warm and soft and giving. So, instead, he kissed the top of her head in the shadows where no one could see them as they waited at the corner to cross the street.

The more she talked about the upcoming weekend, the more he dreaded it. Not because he didn't want to spend the time with her, but because he did. Too much. Before he knew it this would all be over and they'd go their separate ways. There's be no more cuddling in the dark, whispered confessions, or midnight kisses. His life would return to normal and so would hers.

Normal and boring and bland. But he'd deal with it, just like he dealt with everything life had thrown at him so far. He was a survivor, and survivors went on, no matter what.

He couldn't keep Mel in his life, not the way they were now. It was fine. He had his friends, his surrogate family at Victory Vets to keep him company. He'd be fine.

And James was coming home soon too. It would be good to see him. Catch up.

No, he decided. This weekend needed to be the end of his deal with Mel. It was time. They'd have a long, sweet goodbye, then it would be over. That was good. He could get out before he messed things up more. They'd part on good terms. His feelings toward Mel only felt so confusing because they'd spent so much time together over the past few weeks. Things with her weren't that serious.

As they reached his bike and headed home, Adam considered the matter settled. They'd go to Miguel's wedding, have a good time, then he'd tell her he was done.

This weekend would be the end.

CHAPTER TWELVE

That Wednesday, Mel sat in the small computer lab inside the Point Beacon Public Library, scrolling through page after page of cocktail dresses with Lilly during her lunch break.

Even though Lilly had doubts about what Mel was doing with Adam, she was also Mel's best friend and therefore determined to lend her support, in whatever way she could, she'd said.

Mel barely paid attention to Lilly's constant chatter as she looked at dress after dress on her screen, her thoughts circling back to Adam and how oddly he'd acted at dinner the other night. Two had passed since then and she hadn't seen him since, Adam claiming he'd been super busy at work when she'd called him. Apparently, they'd taken on a new engine rebuild project, and now he had his hands full. It was certainly possible, but she still sensed something more lurking beneath the surface of his excuse.

Meanwhile, her parents were busy planning a big joint

birthday party-slash-welcome home shindig for her and James. All of it only made the knots of tension in Mel's stomach tighten even more. This whole thing with Adam would be over soon, then...

What?

Well, honestly, Mel wasn't sure, but she hoped they'd start something new. Maybe try dating out in the open for a change. She knew Adam still had some weird hang-ups about it, but maybe having James back home for him to confide in would help with that. Mel hoped so anyway.

To keep herself from obsessing over things, Mel had put her nose to the grindstone at work, getting things done at the library she'd put off for months because she simply didn't have the time. She'd also taken on several new volunteers from the local retirement center and put them to good use, sorting the stacks and archiving older books in the collection to make room for new acquisitions.

There were even a couple of older gentlemen in the group who didn't mind a little hard labor—if you could call moving empty wheeled bookshelves around "hard labor." They'd helped Mel redesign the layout of the history section to make it more accessible and user-friendly.

But she still hadn't decided what to wear to the wedding in Chicago yet. Which was the other reason Lilly was here. To help her choose wisely and quickly, so she could express-order it for delivery before she and Adam left on Friday after work. As a photographer, Lilly spent her days portraying people in their best light. Mel couldn't think of anyone better to help her find something that would make Adam snap to attention when he saw her.

Unfortunately, it had been nearly an hour of constant searching by Mel and they still hadn't found the perfect dress. She had curves and accentuating those without making her look too voluptuous was a priority.

Mel glanced at the clock, seeing her lunch break was almost over. This was taking too long. She didn't mean to be so picky, but she wanted to look good on Adam's arm, like they belonged together and she wasn't some charity case he'd brought along because she was his best friend's little sister. But maybe she was putting too much pressure on this one garment.

Maybe I'm putting too much pressure on this whole thing period.

The thought made her squirm a little in her seat. Sure, she might have allowed her feelings for Adam to grow deeper than she'd intended, considering their agreement, but that was normal, right? After all, she'd shared her body with him, bared her soul to him. She wanted to keep seeing him after their deal was over.

The problem was, she hadn't told him any of this.

Her newest issue of *Cosmo* had proclaimed, "The only way to lead an authentic, fulfilled life is to take risks. Battle those doubt demons. Your reward could be unexpected and beyond your wildest dreams."

That all sounded sunny and sweet and Hallmark perfect but it hadn't mentioned anything about how to handle a man who was as skittish as a wild colt about anything related to emotions or relationships or true intimacy.

While Mel was usually far too pragmatic to go in for all that basic motivational fluff, even she had to admit her time with Adam had worked for her. She'd come so far in just a few short weeks, both with her outer appearance and her inner desires. And yes, maybe a tiny part of her still clung to her old fears—that she wasn't enough for a guy like Adam and there was no way he'd seriously consider dating her after their deal—she'd effectively countered those negative voices so far. And she was so close to reaching her ultimate goal of being with Adam Foster, her dream man, that stopping now seemed impossible, despite their looming deadline.

She swallowed hard against the lump of anxiety in her throat and scrolled through more photos onscreen. But what she saw in her head was the last night she and Adam had spent together. How she'd woken up with her head on his chest, over his heart, and how she'd lain in the predawn gloom, listening to his soft snores and savoring his heat and the protective weight of his arm slung around her waist. When he was asleep, the constant tension in his body vanished, leaving him looking so young and vulnerable. Adam would hate that, she knew. He had a thing about being vulnerable with people. It was probably why he still clung to his old playboy persona around town when he'd proven to be anything but in her short time with him. She wasn't sure why he feared getting too close with anyone, and a good time to discuss it had never come up for them.

Maybe this weekend would give her an opportunity to ask him.

She sighed and kept scrolling through more dresses.

The rumors about Adam were still going strong in Point Beacon, what with all the groupies that always hung out at Victory Vets and, if the gossip were to be believed, Adam took to bed on a regular basis. He'd denied being with anyone else but her during their agreement when she'd asked him, and part of Mel said it shouldn't matter even if he was seeing other people. Hell, he'd come right out and asked her about it that day at lunch, but still, the thought of him being with another woman made Mel's chest ache.

Which was really dumb because they didn't belong to each other. Not really. And they wouldn't either, not unless Adam made a major change from his "no love" stance and who was she to ask him to?

Ugh. She rubbed her temples at the tiny frustration headache starting there. They had one week left until their deal was over. One week until Mel went back to her books and her cat and her private little single life. Without Adam.

Shoulders slumping, Mel jabbed a last hunk of lettuce from her salad with her fork and shoved it in her mouth, chewing without really tasting it, her appetite gone.

"Wait!" Lilly said from beside her, nudging Mel with her elbow. "Go back one page." Mel did and Lilly gasped, pointing to an image of a deep burgundy knee-length silk chiffon dress with a halter neckline and a full circle skirt. Red was Adam's favorite color, and he said Mel had the best legs in town, so this cocktail dress ticked both those boxes. "It's perfect!" Lilly grinned. "Adam will love it."

Mel shushed her, glancing around to make sure none of the nosy volunteers had overheard. Thankfully, they all seemed to be busy with their tasks.

Lilly gave her an irritated look and waved off Mel's concern. "Whatever. Bring up the size options for the dress. If you go down in flames, might as well look gorgeous as you burn, right?"

"Will you shut up?" Mel snapped, heat prickling her cheeks. "I'm not going down in flames. My plans were a success."

"Uh huh." Lilly looked dubious as she commandeered the computer from Mel to check out the dress herself. "So, Adam is going to give you a happily ever after then?"

"What? No." Mel shook her head, flustered. Had she been that transparent? "I don't want that. I mean, I do, but he doesn't. We had an agreement and I'm sticking to that. It's fine. Stop talking about it."

Lilly shook her head, clicking several more buttons on the screen. "Well, whatever you say, I think you and he are in deeper than either of you think. I know you, Mel. You are not a one-night stand kind of gal. You've got forever written all over you. And for a guy like Adam, that's kryptonite."

The fact Lilly had basically nailed the truth only made Mel feel more exposed. She shoved Lilly out of the way and ordered the dress without even looking at the price, just wanting this conversation to be done. "There. I have my dress. You can go now."

"Yikes. Sorry if I hit too close to the bone, hon," Lilly said, not looking sorry at all. "Like I said, I just don't want to see you hurt when all this is over. Because you know it will be over soon, right?"

Mel snatched up her credit card and shove it back into her purse, avoiding her best friend's gaze. Yes, she knew that. No, it didn't stop it from hurting.

"Thanks for helping me find a dress," she said, ignoring Lilly's other question.

"Hey." Lilly put her hands on Mel's shoulders when she

straightened, forcing her to meet Lilly's gaze at last. "I'm only trying to protect you here, Mel."

"I know." They hugged and when Mel pulled back, she changed subjects. "You're coming to the party next weekend, right? To take pictures of James's homecoming?"

"Yep." Lilly smiled. "Wouldn't miss it."

"Good." Mel closed down the computer then pushed to her feet, glad to have something to discuss that didn't involve Adam. "Maybe you can talk to him about the festival thing with the mayor's office."

"Maybe." Lilly tucked a stray curl of her dark hair behind her ear. "It'll be nice having James back in Point Beacon again."

"Yeah, it will." She still hadn't told her brother about what had happened with her and Adam, but depending on this weekend, she might not need to. If she asked Adam about his past and he told her to get lost, things would be over sooner than expected and there'd be no needed to let anyone else into their little secret.

Little secret.

Lilly was right. Mel didn't do casual sex very well. Then again, before Adam she hadn't done sex at all, so...

"Oh!" Lilly checked her watch and grabbed her purse from the counter. "I need to go or I'll be late for a consultation on a new wedding shoot." She gave Mel another brief hug before hurrying toward the exit. "Call me when the dress comes in and we'll pick out shoes and accessories."

Once her bestie was gone, Mel went back to work, checking out materials for patrons, though her mind still whirled with thoughts of Adam and all the loose ends they still had left to tie. She waited until the last patron walked out before dropping her head into her hands. She needed to just be honest with Adam and tell him how she was feeling.

And if he didn't want a future with her, then she'd let him go.

No matter how it might break her heart.

CHAPTER THIRTEEN

Saturday evening, Adam stood in the opulent ballroom of the luxurious Lakeshore Hotel on Chicago's Michigan Avenue where Miguel's wedding reception was being held.

He'd known Camille's family had money, but he'd never guessed anything like this. From the enormous fresh floral arrangements decorating all the tables, to the small orchestra playing softly in the corner of the gigantic space, it was all like something straight out of a millionaire's dream, with a little Tijuana flair thrown in for flavor by the mariachi band roaming amongst the tables, playing festive music between the orchestra sets.

All this decadence was so far from Adam's reality growing up he didn't even know how to process it. Not to say he wasn't fully enjoying the reception. The whole trip really. Way more than he'd expected to.

They'd made the trip to Chicago in Mel's Camry and once

they'd left the town limits of Point Beacon, it had felt like the restraints and expectations he'd been saddled with his whole life had fallen away. Yes, he was still concerned about how to break Mel's fall when all this was over, but at least, right now, he felt like he had a bit of breathing room for a change.

After they'd checked in at the hotel last night, they'd unpacked then spent the evening alone together, ordering room service and watching the latest superhero movie on pay-per-view.

This morning, they'd gotten up early, showered together, then headed downstairs to enjoy the pre-wedding breakfast put on by Miguel and his fiancée and their families. The whole time Miguel's sister, Gina, had barked out orders to the caterers and the wedding planner, but the yelling seemed to have paid off later, because the ceremony had gone off without a hitch.

Now everyone seemed to be enjoying themselves at the reception.

Adam sat at a table near the wall and watched Miguel twirl his glowing bride in an elegant underarm turn as the bittersweet Mexican waltz they'd chosen for their first dance played. Adam was no fashion expert, but even he could admire the beauty of Camille's traditional Latin-style wedding dress, the white satin fitted expertly through the top and hips then flaring out at the bottom to a hem and train embroidered in bright pink and red flowers. Her baby bump was proudly displayed and both bride and groom had kicked off their shoes long ago to dance barefoot. Adam didn't think he'd ever seen Miguel look happier, and both he and Camille seemed to only have eyes for each other.

A touch of envy mingled with joy in his chest before Adam could stop it, the reflection of his buddy's deep devotion and love for his partner only serving to reflect the distinct lack of it in his own life. He'd always thought being alone meant being safe, but Mel had shown him differently and Adam still didn't know what to do with that.

Since he'd made that deal with her, his days had seemed happy, sunny somehow, but it wasn't real. He knew that, regardless of how he might yearn to make it so.

He had no business being with Mel after their deal. He didn't have the first clue how to have a healthy relationship. He had no clue how to love someone and stick around. So, no.

After this weekend, he'd go back to his ordinary life and make it work. It had been fine a few weeks ago and it would be again. He took a long swig of his beer and swallowed hard.

Even if it felt like he'd have a huge Mel shaped hole in his center.

All the more reason to end it now and be done. That was their deal and he needed to stick to it. He couldn't be *that guy* for her, the knight in shining armor she deserved. He was a player, the town bad boy, the guy you messed around with on your way to forever. Nothing more.

Then a murmur when through the crowd seated near him and Adam turned to see Mel standing in the doorway to the ballroom. She'd insisted on going back to the room to change after the wedding, saying she'd bought a dress better for dancing than the white sheath dress she'd worn to the wedding earlier. So, Adam had come downstairs by himself to stake out their seats.

Now, he drank in the sight of her beauty like fine wine, the air seizing in his lungs. She'd put her hair up again in a messy topknot that revealed her long, graceful neck. As she scanned the room for him, her cheeks were flushed with excitement, and her eyes sparkled with anticipation. When they'd made love last night, Adam had felt a sense of desperation, knowing it would be one of their last times together. He'd let Mel take charge, demanding her pleasure, the memory of her soft cries still setting his body tingling.

Afterward, she'd snuggled into his side and held on tight, like she might never let him go.

He'd do what she couldn't, but later. After the were back in Point Beacon. For now, he couldn't have stopped himself from going to Mel if he'd tried. He stood to walk over to the door to get her, when Camille came up beside him and grabbed his arm. He'd been so distracted my Mel that Adam hadn't even noticed the bride leaving the dance floor.

"Come on," Camille said, tugging him toward the center of the room. "Time for a group dance."

"Wait, I—" He tried to pull free to get Mel, but to no avail. Camille yanked Adam onto the floor and into the middle of a gathered circle of friends and family, including the other guys from Victory Vets and their partners. Mel soon arrived as well, thanks to Miguel, and Adam put his arm around her waist to keep her close, swaying gently to the strains of a Spanish melody he hadn't heard before.

Miguel then took the mic from the orchestra conductor to announce, "Thank you all for being here to celebrate our union. It wouldn't have been the same without all of you." His dark gaze then brightened with tears as he glanced as his beautiful bride. "Camille, *mi corazón*, the mother of my child."

Camille blew him a kiss. "*Mi esposo*"

Then Miguel dropped the mic and ran over to sweep his new wife into his arms and kiss her soundly before raising a glass of champagne in a toast:

"*A todos nuestros amigos, les deseamos amor, salud, dinero y tiempo para disfrutarlos. To all our friends, we wish you love, health, money, and the time to enjoy them. ¡Que vivan!*"

The crowd cheered.

Miguel then pointed at Adam, making his pulse stumble a little. "And you, my friend. You're next."

Adam recoiled before he could stop himself, ignoring Mel's curious look as he covered his reaction with a joke. "I'm not kissing you."

Laughter filled the ballroom.

Miguel gave him a flat look. "You know what I mean. You're the best man I know, Adam Foster, and I wouldn't be here now if you hadn't gotten me through those terrible days during the war. I owe you more than I can ever repay. Thank you, my brother."

They shared an awkward bro hug as Adam struggled to act normally under the scrutiny of the people around them. He felt like a fraud, an intruder here where everyone was in love and happy and worthy. He didn't belong. He needed to go before they figured it out and kicked him to the curb.

Then he turned and found Mel waiting, watching him with heat and hope and obvious affection and he went to her, pulled by some unseen connection, one he didn't understand and one he was sure would disappear as fast as it appeared. As the music started again, Adam pulled her into his arms and swayed with her, shell-shocked and dizzy from feelings he didn't understand and wanted to run and hide from, yet here he was with Mel. Her warmth made him yearn for privacy, so he could remove that frothy bit of nothing she called a dress and pleasure her until he didn't know where she ended and he began. Until neither one of them could let go. They might not have a future, couldn't have one, but they had tonight, and it would have to be enough.

All too soon though, Camille pulled Mel away from him to get a drink at the bar, and Adam watched them walk away, feeling like he'd just lost the most precious thing in his life.

He'd only ever felt that once before, the day his mother walked away.

"She's great, man," Miguel said, slapping him on the shoulder. "Does James know you're in love with his sister?"

"What?" Heart skittering against his ribcage, Adam stumbled back a step. "No. What? No. I don't love Mel. I'm just helping her out and—"

He bumped into several other guests he backed up toward the exit, Miguel's smile morphing into concern.

"Buddy, wait. What's wrong?" Miguel said, following him.

Before Adam could make it out of the ballroom though, Mel returned, taking his arm. "Dance with me."

A sweet, slow ballad had started, the words Spanish, but the angst translated just fine. Adam found himself led back to the dance floor and against Mel's body. The scent of her sweet perfume seemed to penetrate the daze he was in, slowing his pounding pulse as she cuddled closer to him. They fit together so perfectly, not just in bed, but out of it, too.

Does James know you're in love with his with his sister?

Adam closed his eyes. No. He didn't. How could he when Adam just realized it himself. And it was the absolute worst thing that could happen to him. Because it meant he failed.

Failed to protect Mel. Failed to protect himself. Failed to keep their deal. Failed pretty much everywhere, as usual in his life.

His pulse beat like a countdown clock, signaling his impending doom.

"Okay?" Mel asked, looking up at him.

He shook his head because no. He wasn't okay. He never would be again. "Let's go upstairs."

"Okay."

Adam led her off the dance floor and out into the lobby, the elevator ride up to their room a blur. He loved Mel and he shouldn't, couldn't. He wasn't good enough for her, would never be good enough for her.

It didn't stop him from wanting her on a soul deep level.

If this was their last night together, here in this fantasy palace, then he wanted to give her a night so passionate and perfect she'd remember him long after she'd left him behind. It was the least he could do.

It was the only thing he could give her really. He had nothing else.

As they entered their room and made love, every touch, every look, every word, tightened the spring inside him until he shattered completely, giving her everything. Showing her with his actions how much he cared, since he could never say the words.

And afterward, when she fell asleep in his arms, he gathered the shards of his broken heart and tucked them away again in the shadows, just like he'd done all those years ago when his mom left. He'd gone into this with his eyes open, knowing how much he stood to lose and now it was over. Mel was off-limits and his life would go back to normal.

Even if Adam would never look at normal the same way again.

CHAPTER FOURTEEN

Once they were back in Point Beacon Sunday evening, Mel's hand shook as she unlocked her door. Adam had been quiet all day, and she was worried. Last night had been amazing, but she'd not missed the hunted look in his eyes at the reception before they'd left.

They walked inside and Mel flipped on the lights. Her neighbor, Ms. Petronelli had watched Waldo for her but had dropped the cat off earlier, so now the air was filled with loud meows as Waldo twined around both their legs, demanding attention.

"Come in," Mel said, heading down the hall toward the kitchen. "We should talk."

Adam set her bag on the floor in the foyer then closed the door, bending to pick up Waldo before following her down the hall. His face was currently buried in her cat's fur, so she couldn't see his expression, but Mel felt ready to burst from her skin. She hadn't had a chance to talk to him over the weekend about his past and about their future together and now was her last chance.

"Uh, can I get you something to drink?" she asked him.

"No, I'm good thanks." He put Waldo down then took a seat at her island, the same place he'd been when they'd first made their deal.

The deal.

Her stomach flipped before sinking to her toes.

She pulled a can of ginger ale out then set it aside, not really thirsty. She wiped her damp palms on the legs of her jeans then took a deep breath for courage, knowing she needed to get this over with before she couldn't anymore. "Listen, Adam. I—"

"Deadline's up," he said, his tone oddly emotionless. "It's all good."

Mel frowned. "What? No. It's not all good. I know something was bothering you at the reception and I'd like to know what it was." She walked over to sit on the other stool in front of him, reaching out to put her hands on his forearms but stopping when he pulled back. Heart in her throat, she forced herself to continue. "You never talk about yourself, your past. You know that if something's wrong or something triggered you, you can talk to me. Your mom left when you were little, right? James mentioned that once. That must have been horrible for you."

"I really don't want to talk about that," he said, starting to slide off his stool but then realizing she blocked his path. A muscle ticked near his tense jaw. "I need to go, Mel."

"No, you don't," she said, anger inching out her concern. "Why won't you talk to me, Adam? If this is about your mom, you have nothing to be ashamed of. She made her choice to leave and—"

"Stop it," he growled. "You don't know what you're talking about."

"Then tell me," Mel pleaded. "Please. We can't—"

"Can't what?" Adam asked, looking at her now and she wished he wouldn't. Not with his dark eyes hard and full of pain. "Can't be together? Well, that was never going to happen anyway, was it? Not with the deal we made. Not with me being..." He gestured toward himself like it was obvious. "It wouldn't work Mel. Never could. That's why I warned you at the start. I don't do love. Because love doesn't do me."

Stunned, she blinked at him, the dots connecting in her head for the first time. "Adam, that's not true. You are lovable, even if you think you're not."

"Yeah?" His tone had taken on a jagged edge that sliced straight through her. "Stop lying, Mel. You don't love me. You might think you do, but that's not real. I'm just the first guy you slept with, that's all. It doesn't mean anything. You'll find someone else who's better for you, who can give you all the things you need. Someone who isn't me. This is over. We're over. Goodbye."

Those last words hung in the air, lethal as exploded grenades as he got up then and stalked down the hall, the front door slamming behind him with resounding finality.

This is over. We're over. Goodbye.

Mel surprised numbness at his abrupt departure soon gave way to heartache and she pressed her hand against her chest as tears stung her eyes. Well, she should have expected that, shouldn't she?

He's told her from the start not to fall for him and yet she'd gone ahead and done it anyway. She had no one to blame but herself. It was stupid to be upset now.

So, so stupid.

She got up and put the unopened can of ginger ale back in the fridge then leaned her back against it as Waldo meowed plaintively up at her as if sensing her pain.

God, I'm such a fool. A stupid, stupid fool.

Even with all the changes she'd made, even with her new clothes and new look, the guy had still left her behind in the dust. So much for her Pretty Woman fairy tale coming true.

The only way to lead an authentic, fulfilled life is to take risks. Battle those doubt demons. Your reward could be unexpected and beyond your wildest dreams.

Stupid *Cosmo*. She planned to burn that issue at the first opportunity. Just as soon as she found a way to keep functioning with her heart flayed open and left bleeding all over the floor.

Why hadn't she believed him when he'd said at that start that he didn't do love? Why hadn't she stuck with their deal?

She slowly slid down until she was sitting on the floor, her tears finally falling as she went over his answer over and over run her mind. *You'll find someone better for you. Someone who isn't me.*

Except she didn't want anyone else but Adam Foster. Never had.

And even if he didn't want her back, he was it for her. She swiped a hand across her damp cheeks then pulled Waldo in for a hug.

I'm just the first guy you slept with.

True, but that didn't mean that it hadn't been special. Mel might've been a virgin but that didn't mean she was completely inexperienced. She'd had orgasms on her own, but nothing had ever compared to the connection she felt with Adam during that pivotal moment.

She closed her eyes and remembered the night before, their last together. He'd been so intent, so careful, as if memorizing every detail of her in his mind so he could remember later. No way had it been just sex for him either, she'd bet her house on it. He refused to admit because...

I don't do love because love doesn't do me.

Because he was afraid. Her eyes opened at the realization. It was plain as day now. And she'd been right on track with what had happened with his mother too, though she'd gone about it all wrong. She shouldn't have pushed him to reveal more than he was ready to. And now she'd driven him away, just like she'd done with every other guy she'd tried to date.

She had no one to blame but herself.

Seducing her bad boy, making her transformation, getting the life she thought she wanted had been an utter failure, because Mel had ended up being the one seduced in the end. By everything she thought would fulfill her but only ended up leaving her even more empty than before. Alone and sad and hurt beyond belief.

Worse, she'd left Adam wounded too.

Her spirits plummeted even more as she swiped away more tears, angrier at herself than anything. She was stronger than this, darn it. She'd been fine as she was before, and she would be again. They'd had a couple of amazing weeks together, but had been nothing but an illusion, and now it was over.

She'd go back to her library and her boring staid life and forget the rest. Maybe get that promotion she'd wanted. Life would go on.

No matter how impossible that seemed at present.

BY FRIDAY NIGHT, Adam felt like a hot mess. Literally. He swiped his hand across his sweaty forehead, then pulled at the neck of his T-shirt feeling like the thing was strangling him. He should've called off sick and let the rest of the Victory Vets guys pick up James at the airport in Indy, but that would've been a coward move, and Adam wasn't a coward.

Not about most things, anyway.

Besides, he'd missed his best bud a lot and wanted to see him, even if they had an awkward conversation in front of them about what had happened with Adam and Mel. He'd thought about keeping it a secret still, but considering how well he and James knew each other, that wouldn't work. James would know right away something was off with him.

Just like Mel did.

He shook off that unwanted thought. Must be a family trait.

He'd done his best not to think about Mel at all this past week, what had happened on Sunday night still too painful to poke at. Except somehow, after they'd picked up James, they'd ended up at the Tipsy Wench, and all Adam could picture was when he'd been there with Mel.

James kept watching him from across the table, giving him curious looks, but Adam wasn't ready to tell him yet. Hell, he was still trying to understand what had happened with Mel himself.

Jag raised his bottle of ale in a toast. "To the last of us home safe!"

Adam relaxed his death grip on his seltzer water and forced himself to breathe. Jag was right; tonight was about the guys, a celebration of them all being together once more, safe and sound.

"Ya know, James," Jag said, settling back in his seat. "Maybe one of these days, I'll ask your sister out to lunch. If you don't mind."

James's gaze never left Adam as he shrugged, "Why would I mind? It's her business who she dates."

"Cool, bro," Jag said before butting into an argument between one of the other guys and Hollywood about a stunt scene in the latest racing movie at the theater.

Adam, however, felt anything but cool. In fact, heat had surged up inside him at the thought of Mel dating other people, especially someone from the garage. Which was so dumb because Adam had had his shot with her and turned it down. He had no claim on Mel anymore, despite the fact he'd lost his heart to her. For whatever that was worth.

He sighed and scrubbed a hand through his hair.

What a mess he'd made of everything. As usual. Man, he could've really used a beer about now. But he was the designated driver for the group tonight, which was fine with him, since the last thing he needed was to get boozed up and get into a fight because he was hurt over this thing with Mel.

The band broke into a cover of a Guns N' Roses song and everyone at the table got up to dance except him and James.

Once they were alone, James scooted over into Jag's vacant seat and leaned in to ask, "You going to tell me what's bothering you?"

"Nothing's bothering me, dude. Just tired, like I said."

James snorted then took another drink of his ale, watching Adam far too closely for his comfortable. "You are seriously the worst liar ever."

"I'm not lying," Adam said defensively.

"You just don't want to talk about it."

"No, I don't." Scowling, Adam sat forward to rest his elbows on the scarred tabletop. "Can you please just drop it?"

James shook his head, chuckling. "Never thought I'd live to see the day."

Adam growled. "What day?"

"The day you finally fell in love."

He felt like the earth vanished from beneath his feet, and he gripped the edge of the table. Was he that obvious? Christ, he hoped not. Otherwise, all this pain he'd put himself through, keeping this thing with Mel and him in the shadows, sneaking around for weeks, was for naught.

"Who is it?' James asked after a few beats. "Someone I know?"

"What? No." Though Mel's name clawed up his throat and nearly escaped before Adam bit it back. He didn't love Mel. Couldn't, shouldn't love Mel. He wasn't right for her. She deserved so much better than him. He started to stand, needed to move, get some space to work through all this. "I'm getting another water. Want anything?"

James shook his head, waiting until Adam's back was to him to say, "It's Mel, isn't it?"

Adam nearly tripped over his own feet, catching himself on the back of a chair before he toppled to the floor in shock. He turned back to his best friend, hoping his guilt wasn't written all over his face. "Why would you—"

"I didn't think that." James shrugged. "Not for sure anyway. But thanks for confirming my suspicions."

Feeling like all the bones in his body had turned to jelly, Adam slumped back down in his chair, covering his face with his hands. "I'm sorry, James. I didn't mean for it to happen. I was helping her with this crazy project she had. She wanted to change herself, said she was tired of who she was and wanted to be someone different." He left out the virginity part because, well, that was a bit much for best friends to discuss, especially when one of them was Mel's older brother. Still, an odd mix of relief and remorse popped inside him like an overfilled balloon. "I should have told you sooner. I'm sorry I didn't." He exhaled slow. "But it doesn't matter now anyway because it's over."

James looked surprised by that. "She broke up with you?"

He shook his head. "No. I did it. I knew there was no future in it, so I let her go."

"Why was there no future in it?" James asked, frowning.

Adam gave a derisive snort. "Seriously?" He gestured toward himself. "You know my reputation, dude. I'm not made for relationships."

His best friend seemed to take that in a moment as the band switched to a Bon Jovi classic. The rest of their group stayed out on the floor, singing along with the lyrics about living on prayers. Adam could relate.

"Let's talk about your reputation," James said after a while.

"Can we not?" Adam shook his head and downed the rest of his seltzer.

"You've always wanted everyone to think you're a player," James said, ignoring Adam's comment. "But you're not. Not really."

Adam gave him an incredulous stare. "I dated four women at once in high school."

"Dated is an overstatement," James said. "Had sex with them is more accurate, and they knew the score. You weren't shady about it."

"I did not have a foursome, James."

"My point exactly," James countered. "You were a serial dater, but you weren't a player. A player would have used whoever he was with to do whatever he wanted. He would've pitted all those women against each other, gone behind their backs, maybe even had that foursome, if it made you happy. But you didn't. You just refused to get tied down. Why is that?"

Adam did not want to get into that. Not here, not now. But with his best bud staring him down across the table and the cover band switching to a classic Journey power anthem that had everyone crowding around their table and making a quick escape all but impossible, Adam felt he had little choice.

He shook his head. "You know why, man."

For the first time, James looked genuinely confused. "No, I don't. That's why I'm asking."

"Look at me, James," Adam said. "I'm a mess. I can't commit to anyone, I live in a rundown shack, and I have five dollars in my savings account. My family is dead, and when they were alive they weren't exactly Leave It to Beaver. You met my dad. He was scary on a good day. My mom left us because she couldn't take it anymore. I don't blame her. I wouldn't want any part of me either, if I could get away from me. That can't be the kind of man you want your sister involved with. I don't deserve her."

James sat there for a long time, just blinking at him. So long, in fact that Adam began to squirm a little in his seat. Finally, James took a deep breath then asked, "Do you love her?"

"It doesn't matter if I love Mel or not," he grumbled.

"I think it's the only thing that matters," James countered. "Look, I'm sure that whatever I say to you right now won't make a difference. You seem set on seeing yourself as inferior, but dude, you're one of the best people I know." Adam opened his mouth to argue, but James held up a hand, stopping him. "Let me finish. Now, that's not to say you don't have your faults. You're opinionated, cocky, and your wardrobe choices could stand a bit of variety. Plus, I'm getting really tired of constantly having to cheer your grumpy butt up. But... you genuinely care about and want the best for people and you never judge anyone. You accepted me when I came out, no questions asked, and never once treated me any differently. That meant the world to me, Adam. And regardless of your past, being a strong, kind person in this day and age is a miracle. My sister would be lucky to have you as her partner, and we'd be lucky to add you to our family, bro. You need to talk to Mel and work this out." Then he stood and put his ale down on the table as the cover band launched into the classic YMCA. "Now, if you'll excuse me, I need to go have a queer fest for a second before I burst."

Adam sat at the table alone, watching his friends party and laugh and dance, the word 'lucky' pinballing around inside his head. He'd been lucky to find these people, lucky to have their support after growing up with none. He'd been lucky to have Mel too, however briefly.

He missed her more every day, the ache growing into his chest until it felt like a gaping wound, pounding in time with his pulse.

My sister would be lucky to have you as her partner, and we'd be lucky to add you to our family, bro.

His whole life, he'd always wanted to be loved and accepted and James had just offered him that on a silver platter, but Adam still couldn't process it all. Couldn't believe it was true.

Was he making a mistake, walking away from Mel now? Was he using his own insecurities as an excuse to run away?

He'd been a lot of things in his life, but a coward wasn't one of them. Maybe James was right. Maybe he did need to talk to Mel one last time and explain why them being together was a bad idea. Make her understand. Remind himself too.

They'd both be at the party tomorrow, and while Adam didn't want to ruin her birthday, perhaps it was the best time to get it all out in the open once and for all.

CHAPTER FIFTEEN

Mel was up early on Saturday, unable to sleep much the night before. Then again, she hadn't had a good night's sleep since the night Adam had told her it was over.

Waldo was curled into a ball near her feet while Mel sipped her tea, dressed in an old, familiar pink twinset and plain black pants. They were comfortable and helped ground her in a world that felt suddenly precarious.

Through the window above the sink across from her she saw a lovely sunrise developing, all bright purples and golds. Normally, she loved the colors and sense of optimism it brought, but today she took little joy in the dawn, nor the fact it was her twenty-fifth birthday.

The deadline. Her stupid deadline.

She'd had such high hopes for a lasting transformation in her life when she'd started this whole thing, and now she was left with nothing but questions and heartache.

With a sigh, she opened her phone and checked her calendar. Her schedule was full for the day, with Lilly coming over this morning to have a private celebration, then later the big party at her parents' house. It was good, she supposed, staying busy. Kept her from sitting around moping and stewing over what had happened with Adam.

Well, more than she already was, anyway.

At least her interview for the promotion at work had gone well. She'd had her second meeting with the hiring committee over Zoom and they all seemed to like her very much. There was just one more step left before the hiring decision was made and it involved an in-person interview next month. She'd find out if she was chosen for that last step next week.

Mel frowned and glanced at the digital clock on her stove when a knock sounded on the front door. It was barely six a.m. Who would be out this early? Not Lilly. Getting her best friend up before ten on a weekend was a miracle.

When the knock sounded again, Mel's heart jumped into her throat. Nothing good could come from a visitor this early. It was like a phone call in the middle of the night. Weird and unsettling and almost always the bearer of bad news.

For a fleeting second she wondered if it was Adam, but quickly dismissed the idea. It wouldn't be him; he couldn't have been clearer in cutting ties with her last Sunday.

Not to mention he hadn't so much as texted the whole week, so...

I'm just the first guy you slept with, that's all. It doesn't mean anything.

Trouble was, it meant way more than nothing to her.

Maybe she was just as naive as everyone seemed to think she was.

The knocking continued, growing more persistent each second, and Mel finally slid off her stool, careful not to step on Waldo as she walked to the front foyer to answer. Whatever awaited her on the other side of that door she'd face as best she could, because she was a strong, capable woman. Always had been.

If anything, this whole messy situation with Adam had taught her that, at least. She might not want to go on without him, but she would.

She pulled the door open to find Lilly there. Huh.

"Morning, bestie," Lilly said, holding a bag of pastries in one hand, a holder with two Venti coffees in the other, and looking far more alert than Mel had ever seen her at this hour. "Your emergency caffeine-and-sugar infusion has arrived."

Mel blinked at her retreating back as she walked down the hall to the kitchen, thinking she'd need two of whatever Lilly had consumed to get through this day. Hours of acting cheerful and happy while crying inside loomed in front of her and it was almost enough to have Mel crawling back into bed and staying there for days.

While Lilly fussed around the kitchen with the stuff she brought, pulling out a plate for the pastries, along with silverware and napkins, Mel sank back onto her stool and contemplated her bleak future as the town's spinster cat lady. There wasn't enough coffee and sugar in the world for that kind of torture.

"Hey, now," Lilly said, taking the stool beside hers and nudged Mel with her shoulder. "I know you feel like crap right now, but sitting around brooding won't help anything." She pushed Mel's mug of herbal tea out of the way and replaced it with a steaming cup of joe from the local roaster and a home-made glazed doughnut on a napkin, then added a bear claw nearly as big as Mel's head. "This seems like a two-roll kind of emergency."

"I'm not hungry." Mel dropped her head into her hands, covering her face. "I just want this day to be over with. My life is over."

Waldo meowed loudly, wanting his breakfast too, and Lilly got up to get it for him. "Don't be silly. Maybe things didn't work out with Adam, but you'll meet someone else."

"I don't want to meet anyone else, Lilly," Mel said. "That's the problem. I know you warned me, but I went and fell for him anyway."

Lilly set Waldo's food on the floor for him, then took her seat again, putting an arm around Mel. "I'm so sorry, sweetie."

Mel sobbed into her shoulder, feeling like an idiot. "I thought he'd changed. I thought he cared for me too. But he said I just felt that way because he was the first guy I slept with. He doesn't think he's good enough for me."

"Well, he's an idiot then," Lilly said, rubbing her back then offering Mel a paper napkin to blow her nose in. "Sex is different for men."

"Gee, thanks. That explains it all." Mel blew her nose then swiped the back of her hand across her damp cheeks. "I've had a crush on him since high school."

"I know that too. And so did he."

"Oh, great." Mel thew her hands up, exasperated. "No wonder he thinks I'm pathetic."

"Did he say you were pathetic?" Lilly scowled.

Mel huffed out a breath. "No. He said I was wonderful, actually."

"Good." Lilly ate a bite of her own doughnut. "Because otherwise I'd have to kick his butt at the party later and that would just be embarrassing for everyone. So, he thinks you're wonderful, but he can't be with you. Why?"

"Like I said, he doesn't think he's good enough." Mel shrugged, sniffling. "And no matter what I said, he wouldn't believe me."

Lilly nodded, then was quiet for a beat or two before saying, "Sometimes it's hard, believing the good things people say about you, especially when all you've heard growing up is the bad."

Mel toyed with the napkin in her hands, wincing on behalf of her friend. "I know his childhood wasn't good. James talked about it a couple of times. His dad was pretty awful."

"His dad was an alcoholic and abusive," Lilly said, after swallowing a gulp of latte. "After his mom ran off, Adam was left to take the brunt of that. I remember child protective services showing up at his house a couple of times after his dad got arrested and thrown in jail for public indecency."

"Oh, wow." Mel frowned. "I don't remember that stuff."

"We were pretty young then, but my house was closer to his than yours was back then." Lilly shrugged, polishing off the last bite of her doughnut before continuing. "Adam had to grow up fast and learn to take care of himself because no one else was around to do it for him. And unless he wanted to get shipped off into foster care, he had to cover for his dad too. So he did.

But growing up with that kind of trauma doesn't exactly lend itself to having a healthy self-image."

"No, it wouldn't," Mel said, still processing everything she'd just learned. She'd always suspected there was a lot more going on beneath Adam's surface, even back in high school. That his slick exterior covered something dark and deeply painful, but he'd never once opened up to her. Not even recently when they'd been together. Knowing Adam, it was a combination of him being embarrassed about what happened and also wanting to protect her.

I don't do love because love doesn't do me.

Did Adam really believe he wasn't deserving of her love?

The thought broke her heart.

"People like Adam who've been through so much, they build up defenses, stay guarded, keep people from getting too close because to them being vulnerable means getting hurt." Lilly wiped her mouth then turned slightly to face Mel. "But I will say that I've never seen him open up as much with anyone as he did with you the past few weeks. If I didn't know better, I'd almost think he was happy."

Mel took a huge bite of doughnut, not caring about the flecks of sugar falling on her front as she chewed. "He was happy, I think. We both were. But then he got scared, when we went to that wedding in Chicago. Something must've spooked him. Or maybe it just showed him what he felt like he could never have. After that is when he ended things."

As she ate her doughnut then half her bear claw without really tasting them, Mel ran back through their time together, now seeing it in a different light based on the information Lilly had given her about Adam's childhood. The day at the mall when she'd had her hair and makeup done, then they'd gone shopping. The night he'd taken her to the Tipsy Wench, then they'd made love the first time afterward. The wedding weekend in Chicago. Where she'd seen only joy and discovery and possibilities for the future, Adam must've been reminded over and over of his past and things he thought he didn't deserve.

"I'm so stupid," Mel groaned, feeling awful about it all. "It's all my fault."

"Sweetie, you didn't know." Lilly handed her another napkin as Mel's tears started anew. "Plus, Adam is a grown adult now. Everyone eventually has to take responsibility and fight back if they want things to get better. You can't change him or make him want it. That has to come from him. Just like your transformation had to come from you."

Mel blinked at her best friends. Lilly could be vapid and shallow and flighty sometimes, especially when it came to men, but then other times she was so profound it took Mel's breath away. That's why she loved her so much.

"So, how do we get past this?" Mel asked, rubbing her now pounding temples. "Can we get past this?"

At least Waldo seemed content now, his plump, fluffy body stretched out beside the island in a post-meal food coma. Silence stretched between them.

"You can get past anything, if you both want to." Lilly's expression turned thoughtful. "Having James home might actually help your situation. He and Adam are close, and he'll give Adam someone to talk to about all this. I know confiding in my bestie always helps me."

"Maybe." Mel shifted on her stool, taking a deep breath.

"But they're also partners in Victory Vets and Adam might worry about messing that up too. I know he mentioned it when he was helping me. His whole life is that garage now, and he doesn't want to lose it."

Lilly scoffed. "C'mon. We both know James won't let that happen."

"True. He loves that place as much as Adam." Mel smiled for the first time in days. "Are you sure Adam's coming to the party this afternoon?"

"Where else would he be?" Lilly asked, giving Mel an incredulous look. "The garage is closed in honor of James's homecoming, so unless he wants to sit home alone in that box of a house of his, he'll be there. What time are you due at your parents' house?"

Mel glanced at the clock again. "Noon. Why?"

"Well, you need to get ready," Lilly said, heading toward Mel's bedroom.

"I am ready."

"Uh, no. You're not." Lilly shook her head. "I thought you burned those twinsets."

"I did not!" Mel fussed with her sweater. "These are perfectly good clothes."

"Maybe if you're ninety." Lilly yanked open her closet doors and began going through her things. "Seriously, Mel. Don't let this whole ordeal be for naught. Let's get you glammed up and win you the man you love."

"But—" Mel dug in her heels as her best friend grabbed her arm to yank her forward. "I thought you said you can't force someone to change if they don't want to."

"No one's forcing anything," Lilly said as she tugged off

Mel's cardigan and tossed it on the bed behind them. "You're just going to show Adam what's he's missing."

"Pretty sure he's already well aware of that," Mel grumbled as Lilly tugged her into the bathroom.

"We'll see about that." Lilly jammed on the shower then returned to the door. "Take a nice hot shower while I pick out a new outfit for you."

"But I already took a shower," Mel called as the door started closing behind Lilly.

Lilly stuck her head back in and gave her a quick once-over, then shook her head. "Nope. Definite do over. Go!"

Mel was too exhausted to argue anymore and even she had to admit the warm water felt nice. As she stood under the spray, letting it soothe away her aches and pains from another sleepless night, she wished she didn't have to go to the party. Wished she could go back and never forced Adam to make that deal with her. Not because he hadn't helped her but because he had. So much, despite his own pain. She'd been so selfish and blind to what he must've been going through. Granted, she had tried to talk to him about it, but he'd closed her off. Unfortunately, she wasn't sure how to get past his walls now, or even if he wanted her to. Which meant she had to go to the party this afternoon to see him.

She had to talk to Adam about all this, once and for all.

ADAM SAT in the office at Victory Vets on Saturday morning, staring at the blank white wall across from him and wondering exactly when his life had gotten so out of control.

Since the place was closed today, he thought he'd get some work done in the office, catch up on the unopened mail and bookkeeping that had gotten away from him the past few weeks since he'd been busy with Mel.

Mel.

His chest ached from missing her, but he forced his attention back to the stack of receipts and ledgers in front of him. Better to think about that than how his head throbbed because he'd had too much to drink the night before.

Growing up with an alcoholic father should've been enough to warn him off booze forever, and up until the last couple of days it had been—except for the occasional ale when he went out socially—but not now apparently.

God, what a freaking mess.

James had been blowing up his phone since the other night, asking if he was okay, but Adam wasn't ready to get into it with him again.

He exhaled slowly and scrubbed a hand over his face, the rough stubble on his jaw scratching his palm. The best thing for him to do right now was put Mel out of his head and his heart and move the hell on. He'd made his choice and now he had to live with it.

Like at the party today. He didn't want to go. Had seriously considered getting out of town so he didn't have to go, but then James would probably send the state police searching for him and it would become a whole thing and Adam didn't need anything else to deal with, so he stayed. And waited. Like a condemned man on death row.

He loved the Bryants. Always had. But their happiness and perfect family felt like salt in a wound today. From the first time he'd met them as a kid, they'd taken him in as one of their own, rallying around him in times of trouble, always having his back.

But now, after lying to them for weeks about what was going on with Mel, then having James call him out last night about it all (truthfully, but still), it was just too much.

He shook his head and glanced at his reflection in the mirror on the wall beside him, cringing. Man, if he was going to be around Mel's parents later, he really needed to do a better job of hiding his feelings about her because right now they were written all over his haggard face, what with the soulful eyes and the dark circles beneath them. He looked like one of those sad clown kid paintings, which was not what you wanted to bring to a joyous celebration.

Here lies the heart of Adam Foster. Gone but not forgotten.

With a sigh, he sat back and opened his top desk drawer, pulling out a small black box with a gold-gilt logo atop it from the jewelry store in the lobby of their fancy hotel in Chicago. He opened it and stared at the golden heart pendant with its lone sparkling diamond inside. Man, if that didn't scream how far gone he was, nothing would.

He'd bought it the morning of the wedding, thinking he'd give it to Mel to wear at the reception, as sort of graduation present for all she'd accomplished. But then she'd kicked him out so she could change and he'd gone on ahead downstairs before her, and...

I don't do love and love doesn't do me either.

Growing up he'd clung to those cheesy shows on TV with their happily-ever-afters, thinking someday he'd find that himself. But the older he got, the more he knew that wasn't true. Love was for the good people, the worthy people. Not for poor suckers like him.

Then Mel had come along with her adoring looks and puppy dog loyalty toward him and he hadn't known what to do with that. He closed his eyes and remembered her following him around and how he'd felt ten feet tall whenever she was around. And even though he'd never had admitted it back then, he'd treasured that more than any other gift she could've given him. With Mel he'd felt like someone, like he mattered. So, when she'd asked him to help her a few weeks ago, of course he'd send yes. It had never really been a question that he would, regardless of what he'd told himself at the time. It was like she'd always seen past his carefully cultivated bad boy exterior, to the real, flawed, vulnerable, wounded man beneath and she loved him anyway. She'd made him feel good and true and worthy.

She'd made him feel like maybe someday he could actually be the guy she always thought he was.

He sighed and opened his eyes, closing the jewel box in his hands.

All that was shot to crap now, and he'd fired the bullet himself.

You don't love me. You might think you do, but that's not real. I'm just the first guy you slept with, that's all. It doesn't mean anything. You'll find someone else who's better for you, who can give you all the things you need. Someone who isn't me.

For those few brief weeks with her, he'd glimpsed what his future might have been if he wasn't so screwed up. For that, and for all the wonderful moments they'd spent together, he'd be eternally grateful.

He supposed that was the real reason he'd bought that

necklace for her. As a symbol of what they'd shared. And now it sat on his desk, looking as forlorn as he felt.

The sound of a key scraping in the lock on the entrance door across the garage jarred him out of his pity party and had him leaning slightly to see who was coming in. Probably Jag. That guy always seemed to forget something here at work...

"Jag? That you?" He called as footsteps drew closer. Then James stuck his head in the office. "We need to talk."

If that wasn't the understatement of the century, Adam didn't know what was. Still, he wasn't really in the mood for a chat at present. "Any chance we can do this later? I'm not feeling the best right now."

"I can see that," James said, plopping down in the chair across the desk from Adam. "I've been thinking a lot about you and Mel."

Great. That made two of them.

Adam let his head fall back, and he looked up at the ceiling as his gut twisted tight. "Look, in case I didn't make it clear the other night, I never meant for it to happen. She came to me one night with the makeover idea and the lessons on flirting, and I knew if I hadn't helped her, she would've recruited someone else, and I didn't want her to get hurt, so I said yes. And I ended up hurting her myself. But what choice did I have? She can't end up with some guy like me, James. You know that."

He felt raw and achy and way too vulnerable. Ever since he'd been a kid, he kept his back to the wall, never letting anyone too close, never letting his guard down. Except with Mel. And James. They were the only people he ever felt totally comfortable with. He trusted them.

James gave a long-suffering sigh, shaking his head. "Dude, I don't know that at all. Which part of our conversation the other night did you not understand? I can't imagine anyone I'd want with my sister more. And you love her. I know you do. I can see it all over that sappy look on your face."

Adam scowled and looked away. "Well, it doesn't matter how I feel anymore because it's over. I ended it. She's free to move on to the next lucky guy and I can get back to my regular life again. The end."

James snorted. "The end, huh? Have you ever met Mel? Once she makes up her mind about something, no way is she letting it go. And that includes you, buddy."

His phone buzzed and he glanced at the screen to see a calendar reminder about the party that afternoon. He should've gotten on his bike and ridden until he ran out of gas, then spent the night far away from Point Beacon, far away from Mel, far away from his past and his heartache and all his mistakes.

He'd lost count of the number of times he'd picked up his phone to call Mel, then stopped. He'd even gone so far as to stroll up the street on his lunch break, past the library, just to try and catch a glimpse of her through the windows. It was silly, since he knew it would never work between them. Still, his heart squeezed tight with regret.

Adam glanced across the desk to see James still watching him, his gaze narrowed now and his expression unreadable. Whatever he had in mind now, Adam doubted he had the energy for it. He'd never felt so low and that was saying something for a kid who used to get beaten up every day at school because of where he lived and how he lived. He'd battled one thing or another for most of his life, and he was so damned tired of fighting.

"Can we please drop this?" Adam asked, weary to his bones.

"No. We can't." James said, sitting forward. "Because the two people I care most for in this world are hurting. You're my business partner and my best friend. When I first came out you were the first person who welcomed me with open arms, no judgment, no questions. And Mel's my sister. We're blood. I won't let either of you ruin your lives because you're too stubborn or blind to see the truth."

"What truth?" Adam asked before he could stop himself.

"That love isn't something you earn. It's a gift, freely given, and if you're lucky enough to find it then hang on tight and never let go." James took a deep breath, staring down at the desktop. "After you got sent home from deployment, there was a firefight, outside one of the villages near our base camp. We'd gone there to patrol the area." He closed his eyes. "The enemy snipers came out of nowhere. It was pitch black. We barely had time to take cover. Three guys didn't make it." His breath caught, and he swallowed hard. "All I could think about, huddled in the dark, scared out of my mind, was everyone back here in Point Beacon. About my family, and you, and Victory Vets. And I vowed to protect it all with everything I had."

Startled, Adam blinked at him, taking that in. "A firefight? Why didn't you tell me?"

James sat back, giving a sad little snort. "Because I didn't want anyone to worry. I'm Mr. Perfect around here, right? It should take more than one little gun battle to shake my soul. Except that night I nearly lost it. Talk about shellshocked."

"Oh man. I'm so sorry." Adam leaned forward resting his forearms on the desk. "You should cut yourself some slack. And

I hate to tell you this, James, but you're not perfect. No one is. Your reaction to that firefight was the normal one. Trauma is trauma."

James cocked his head. "True. So doesn't that apply to you as well?"

Those words set Adam back a few paces. "What?"

"You heard me. Trauma is trauma. Your reaction to what happened to you as a kid made you who you are today, but you can change. Will it be easy? No. But nothing worthwhile is." He stared out the window beside the desk. "But you're the best man I know, Adam. You're my brother by choice. The fact you've spent your life thinking you're less than dirt hurts me because I know it's not true. You've had my back more times than I can count. You work harder than anyone I know, and you're loyal to a fault. And if you're making me say all these nice things to you and then you don't make up with Mel? I'll kick your ass."

Given the absurdity of the conversation, Adam couldn't help but laugh. "I do love Mel. More than anything. But it's up to her if she wants me back."

"Right." James stood and came around the desk to pull Adam into a quick bro hug before he could react. "Welcome to the family. For real this time."

"Uh..." He coughed once James let him go, uncomfortable as his mind began swirling again, from joy or overwhelm this time, he wasn't sure. "Thanks, but we still don't know what she's going to say."

Maybe James was right. Maybe his past didn't have to equal his future. Maybe he could change.

Mel had been a ray of pure light in his dreary life, and he'd do anything to get her back. Even become the man she thought he was, a man she could be proud of. Honestly, he'd gladly slay any dragon, no matter how difficult or painful, as long as Mel was by his side.

"You're coming to the party later, right?" James asked from the doorway.

"Yep." Adam nodded. He had a lot to think about and a lot of plans to make before then though. "I'll see you then."

CHAPTER SIXTEEN

Mel smiled and nodded at the appropriate times as she made her way through the food line, but all she could really see was the fact that Adam wasn't there.

Damn. She'd really hoped he'd come, if only for James.

The air smelled of grilled meat and suntan oil, and classic rock music boomed through the air as people splashed in the backyard pool, beers and cocktails in hand. Tables had been set up on the grassy lawn, covered in cheap plastic tablecloths in various pastel shades, each centered with a large picture of one of the M&M's characters. Huge jars of each color were set up on a separate buffet table in a do-it-yourself mixing station. Mel had filled an entire bowl with green ones, not that it mattered now.

She was being a horrible party hostess and should probably come up with some excuse, faked an illness, anything really to leave early, even if it was her birthday.

But James wasn't there yet, and it would look weird if

neither of them were in attendance, so she stayed and tried to look happy.

Mel glanced up to find Jag looking at her expectantly and realized he'd asked her something, but she had no idea what. Her face felt way too hot and tight as she smiled. "Sorry. I didn't hear your question."

Jag smiled and shook his head. "No worries. You seem a little distracted today."

"I am." Mel set her plate down to smooth a hand down the front of her raspberry-pink dress. She'd bought it the day she and Adam had been shopping in Indy and Lilly had thought it would be a good visual reminder to him of their happier times together. The material was a slinky rayon and the skirt hit her at the knees. She still insisted on wearing a lightweight pink cropped cardigan over the tank-style bodice and added her grandmother's pearls. Lilly had fluffed her hair out into the original style Marguerite had given her, but Mel had pinned the sides back with a pair of pink rhinestone barrettes she'd gotten at her favorite local vintage store.

Going forward, she planned to mix things up, wear her new stuff and her old clothes in different quirky combinations because that's what suited her best. Comfy, cute, quirky chic.

She hazarded another glance at the entrance, but still no Adam.

Stop it. Stop looking. Stop wishing. Stop hoping for things that will never happen.

He'd moved on. She should, too.

But sometimes, at night, she'd swear she could still hear Adam's voice in the kitchen, still smell his cologne in the hall, still feel him beside her as she slept. Even Waldo hovered near the front door now, as if waiting for Adam to walk in and give him a good scratch behind the ears.

It was all made her feel so sad and pointless and pathetic.

Her life had gone back to the way it had been before except now she knew what she was missing. Adam. She was missing Adam.

Thankfully, Jag didn't seem fazed by her melancholy. He just smiled and asked, "Want to have lunch sometime, Mel?"

"Oh, uh..." Nice as his offer was, her heart wasn't in it. "I'm pretty busy at the library right now."

"Shot down in flames in less than five minutes," Hollywood said from a nearby table where the rest of the crew from Victory Vets were sitting. "Ouch, dude. That must be a new record."

Unperturbed, Jag just laughed and took a seat with his comrades. "Hey, you miss one hundred percent of the shots you don't take."

Mel sighed and tuned them out, picking up her plate and carrying it over to an empty table under a large umbrella in the corner. She wasn't the best company right now and Lilly hadn't returned yet either since running home to change. She just started pushing around a mound of potato salad with her fork when a murmur started through the crowd, followed by cheer from the Victory Vets crew.

James had arrived.

He said hello to his friends then made a beeline for Mel, kissing her on the cheek before taking a seat across from her at the table. "Happy birthday, sis. Quarter of a century under your belt now. I'm impressed."

"Thanks." She tried to eat some of her food but had no appetite. "Have you seen Adam?"

"Actually, I have," he said, perking her right up. "He's on the porch out front, waiting for you."

"He is?" She knew she was gaping at him, but her brain was still trying to wrap around the fact that Adam was there, and he wanted to see her.

James grinned, his tawny blond hair glinting gold in the sunshine. He still hadn't found his someone special since coming out before going into the Army, and she really hoped he did. "Go get him, sis."

Mel was on her feet and racing around the side of the house before she even realized what she was doing. She barely noticed Gus MacMillan standing there, discussing the finer points of homemade pickles with her dad, or the curious looks both men gave her.

She stopped fast as she rounded the next corner to the front of the house on the covered porch. The afternoon sun cast long shadows, and flies buzzed everywhere. The humidity wasn't doing her hair any favors, but Mel didn't care. Not with Adam here, not with another chance to win his heart. He looked tired and so beautiful she couldn't breathe. He held a small black box in his hands, his fingers shaking slightly, as if he was as nervous to see her again as she was him. Near his feet sat a jar of green M&Ms.

God, she'd missed him.

When he looked over and saw her, Adam cleared his throat and held out the black box to her. "Melody Bryant, I searched the whole of the hotel jewelry boutique in Chicago to find you the perfect gift. Perfect, just like you."

Time seemed to slow as she took it from him, opening it to reveal a gorgeous necklace with a delicate gold heart pendant attached, one tiny diamond sparkling rainbow-bright in the sun. "Adam, I—"

"Wait." He stepped forward and took her free hand in his, and tears blurred Mel's eyes. Here was the man she loved—the man she'd always loved—on her parents' front porch, at her birthday party, and he'd bought her a necklace and her favorite candy and...

"Mel, I'm sorry about what I said. I was scared and it wasn't true and I love you. I never thought I'd say those words again, but I do. I know I'm an idiot and I hurt you and I still have a lot of baggage from my past I need to deal with, but if you give me another chance, I promise I won't walk away again." He took a deep breath. "Please give me another chance, Mel. Not because I deserve it, but because you are the kindest, most generous person I've ever met known. I'd tell you I want to protect you, but you don't need that. I'd tell you I want to take care of you, but you don't need that, either. So, how about we protect each other, take care of each other and I promise to keep you in green M&Ms for as long as you let me."

She sniffled then hugged him tight. "I love you too, Adam. Always have, always will. You're the best man I know."

When they finally pulled apart, Adam grinned then took the box from her to put the necklace on her. "Does this mean you'll help me ruin my playboy reputation by being my girlfriend?"

Mel laughed, full for happiness for the first time in forever. "I will."

They kissed then, slow and sweet, as Mel traced trembling

fingers down his handsome cheek, her heart swelling with so much love she thought it might burst.

Afterward, she leaned her forehead against his and whispered. "I've loved you since I was fourteen years old, Adam." She touched the necklace gingerly, afraid this might all be a dream. "You've always had my heart, and you always will."

Applause and cheers echoed from the crowd of party guests who had gathered on the front lawn without them noticing, including James and her parents and all the guys from Victory Vets.

Adam pulled her closer and chuckled in her ear, making her shiver with pleasure. "Guess we're officially a couple now, huh?"

"Guess so." Mel pulled back to beam at him, not caring for once that the entire town knew her business. "And as your girlfriend, I'm telling you right now that your bad boy days are over."

The crowd cheered again, and Mel buried her face at the base of Adam's neck, exactly where she always wanted to be.

He kissed the top of her head, saying again, "I love you so much, Mel. I'll do whatever's necessary to make you happy. I promise."

"And I promise," she cupped his cheeks, meeting his dark gaze, "that you already make me happy. Just the way you are."

TWO MONTHS LATER...

• • •

"*WAR AND PEACE* and *Fifty Shades of Grey*," Adam said, peering over Gus MacMillan's shoulder as he waited in line to see Mel at the circulation desk. "Both interesting choices."

"Mind your business, young man," the old coot said. "Mind your business."

Fair enough. Adam bit back a grin and resumed his waiting.

Honestly, his business was pretty awesome right now anyway, both at the garage and in his personal life. He'd moved in with Mel about a week after the party, at her insistence and, just this past week, he'd finally put his dad's old house on the market. It seemed silly to maintain two residences when they spent every spare moment at her place anyway. Plus, it allowed him to shut the door on that part of his past once and for all. Win-win.

And Mel was doing great at the library too. She'd gotten her promotion to regional manager and now oversaw several branches in different towns around the area. One week a month she drove around to all of them for on-site visits, then handled it all online otherwise. Sometimes, if he could get the day off, he'd drive her on his Harley.

He leaned to the side slightly to catch sight of his girl, working with another patron. She looked so good. Truthfully, she'd always looked beautiful to him, but she'd really seemed to have settled into her new style now, blending some of her old things in with the new stuff she'd bought that first day they'd spent in Indy. She was wearing pants today—she did that a lot more now—and they fit her like a second skin.

"Hey, Adam," Lilly said as she buzzed past him with her camera. "Ogling your girlfriend again?"

She was working on a new project for the mayor, something

called the Point Beacon Improvement Project. He'd heard James on the phone the other day too with someone from the town council about it and the Autumn Festival. As long as he didn't rope Adam into helping with whatever he was doing, Adam was fine with it.

The line moved forward, and Adam got a better view of Mel's top half now. She'd worn a form-fitting, low-cut white shirt and a short black cardigan with little red embroidered hearts. And, of course, her heart necklace. Adam's chest squeezed hard with sweetness.

Finally, old Gus stepped up to the desk with his books and Mel scanned them out for him then handed him his slip. "Happy reading, Mr. MacMillan."

The older man grunted and tucked the books under his arm, then headed for the automatic doors at the exit just as Lilly walked up to the desk and cut in front of Adam. "Hey, girl," she said to Mel. "Where's the planning meeting going to be?"

"The main conference room," Mel said, pointing toward a doorway just past the brightly colored children's section. "James is in there already, I think."

"Cool." Lilly swiveled back to look at Adam then back to Mel. "You two have fun."

"Always," Adam said, his gaze never leaving Mel as Lilly left and he stepped up to the counter at last. "Hi."

Mel gave him a quick peck for discretion's sake, then smiled. "What are you doing here? I thought your schedule was full today at the garage."

He gave a nonchalant shrug. "It is, but a guy still needs a break."

"Hmm." Mel eyed him suspiciously. "A break, huh?"

There was no one waiting behind him and no one around to see them, so he took advantage and came around the desk and slid his arms around Mel's waist, holding her just like he'd wanted to since they'd parted that morning. Seemed once he'd opened up to her and let his emotions free, there was no stopping them. He leaned in closer, and kissed her nose just because he could.

A couple kids who were arriving for the daily reading sessions giggled as the passed by, pointing and whispering at Adam and Mel, and damn if he couldn't stop grinning now. "I want one of those someday."

Mel gaped at him. "You do? You never mentioned it before."

He shrugged and looked back at her. "I didn't know until now. After what I went through, I wasn't sure, but yeah. I want a kid someday. With you. What do you think?"

She blinked at him, looking stunned, then elated. "Yes, I want kids too. Three to be exact, though we've never discussed it."

"Okay," Adam said. "What about marriage?"

"Uh," Mel stammered, apparently at a loss for words. "Are you proposing?"

"Do you want me to?" He nuzzled her ear and kissed her neck. He hadn't been entirely honest with her when he'd said he came here on a break. In reality, he'd come here with a very specific purpose in mind. Adam kissed along her jaw to her mouth, then pressed his lips to hers for a long moment. When he finally pulled back, they were both breathless. "Look, Mel. I know we said we wouldn't rush into anything, but I've waited so long to feel this way about someone and when it's right, it's right. So..." He kissed her again, then got down on one knee, pulling a small black velvet box from the pocket of his jeans, then opening it to reveal the sparkling diamond solitaire ring inside. "I love you, Melody Bryant, and I want to spend the rest of my life with you. Will you be my wife?"

Tears glistened in her lovely eyes now as she covered her mouth with shaky fingers. "Oh, Adam. I love you, too. Yes, I'll marry you."

Whoops and whistles and applause went up from the crowd that had gathered around them. Just like at the party, Adam hadn't even noticed. Whenever he was around Mel, his world narrowed to just her.

After slipping the ring on her finger, Adam stood and kissed Mel once more. "Love you."

Mel smiled through her happy tears. "Love you, too, my bad boy."

ABOUT THE AUTHOR

Traci is a USA Today Bestselling romance author and has an MFA in Writing Popular Fiction from Seton Hill University. She writes sometimes funny, usually awkward, always emotional stories about strong, quirky, wounded characters overcoming past adversity to find their forever person. She believes Love is Love and hopes to accomplish brave, beautiful things with her one wild and precious life.

Represented by Jill Marsal at Marsal Lyon Literary Agency, LLC

Enjoy this book and want to chat about it?
Join Traci's Reader Lounge on Facebook!

ALSO BY TRACI DOUGLASS

Harlequin Medical Romance

Anchorage Mercy World:

One Night with the Army Doc

The Nurse's Holiday Goal (NL-exclusive)

Finding Her Forever Family

Weekend with Her Fake Fiancé

First Response In Florida Duet:

The Vet's Unexpected Hero

Her One-Night Secret

Wyckford General Hospital Quartet:

Single Dad's Unexpected Reunion

An ER Nurse to Redeem Him

Her Forbidden Firefighter

Family of Three Under the Tree

Standalones:

A Mistletoe Kiss for the Single Dad

Their Hot Hawaiian Fling

Neurosurgeon's Christmas to Remember

Costa Rican Fling with the Doc

Island Reunion with the Single Dad

Their Barcelona Baby Bombshell

A Mistletoe Kiss in Manhattan

The GP's Royal Secret

Home Alone with the Children's Doctor

Sweet Small Town Romance

Point Beacon Novels:

How to Seduce a Bad Boy

Heavenly Falls Novels:

Worth the Wait

Spicy Paranormal/Romantasy

The Revelation Files:

Flesh & Fate

Blood Ravagers Trilogy:

Blood Bound

Blood Freed

Blood Vowed

Blood Strong (NL-exclusive)

Standalone Short Stories:

When Hermes Met Eos

A Dream to Build a Kiss On

The Griff, the Witch, and the Warlock (NL-exclusive)

SNEAK PEEK OF WORTH THE WAIT

"I'm sorry. We need someone more... *viral.*" The casting director's voice boomed through the cramped audition space. "Next!"

Mandy Reynolds mumbled her thanks to the panel and yanked the glitter-encrusted antennae off her head, along with several long strands of blond hair. Her first real audition back in her hometown and she couldn't book a stupid hand sanitizer commercial—even dressed as a jumbo-size germ.

She'd worn the costume, thinking it might help make her more memorable to the directors, in a good way. Guess she'd been wrong.

Disappointment burned alongside the grief in her chest as she made her way toward the exit, but she did her best to stay positive. She came by her optimism naturally, courtesy of her mother.

Think positive. Better things are just around the corner.

Today, though, the words brought a fresh sting of tears to

Mandy's eyes instead of hope to her heart. Her mom had passed a month prior, after a vicious battle with cancer, and things were still getting settled with the estate. That was the whole reason she was back in Heavenly Falls, to make sure her mother's final wishes were carried out. After her mom's valiant fight against a deadly disease, the least Mandy could do was keep her chin up after blowing an audition. If she didn't get this job it was because it wasn't meant for her. Yes, she needed the money, but there would be another way.

Please let there be another way.

Problem was, she'd been staying with her half sister, Gina, for the past four weeks and worried about wearing out her welcome. Gina hadn't said anything, but Mandy didn't like to stay in one place too long. Too confining. Too risky.

Her phone buzzed in the pocket of her duffel bag, and she pulled it out to find a reminder of her next appointment—a tour of the house on the rental property she'd inherited from her mother. Well, half of it, anyway. The other half her mom had bequeathed to a man Mandy hadn't seen in thirteen years. A guy who'd once made her quake with lust in her Chuck Taylors. A real-life Prince Charming who'd whisk her away to happily ever after.

She'd been wrong about that, too.

Fingers trembling, she clicked off the phone. Was this the break she needed? Mom must've intended for her to sell it for the cash, right? That's the only thing she could figure, since Mandy's traveling lifestyle wasn't exactly conducive to home ownership. The thing she couldn't understand, though, was why her mother had gotten Alex involved. As far as Mandy knew, her mom hadn't had any contact with him since divorcing his father over a decade prior. It made no sense, but then neither did her mom's serial marriages.

Each man had seemed like a good fit for her mother and been kind and generous, but it had never been enough, apparently.

The irony wasn't lost on Mandy. She loved her mom and missed her terribly, but she wasn't like her. Not that way, at least. She moved around because of her work. She didn't like to get involved too deeply with anyone, because long-distance relationships were difficult. It had nothing to do with her nomadic childhood.

Dull numbness spread outward from her core as she ran outside into the gray autumn rain and made a beeline for an Uber idling near the curb. Clambering into the backseat, her bulky costume made the fit precarious. "Eight-two-five West Concord Lane, please."

Minutes later, Mandy climbed out onto the rain-slicked pavement on the outskirts of town. Mr. Pickett, her mother's attorney, stood there sharing an umbrella with a taller man.

Alex. Her ex-stepbrother. Still gorgeous as ever, darn him.

Mandy forced her attention to the Victorian-style house behind them. Not a total disaster, but not exactly *Architectural Digest* material, either. The exterior paint on the gingerbread trim was peeling, and the wraparound porch sagged in one corner. Overall, in need of TLC, but habitable.

"Nice outfit," Alex said, looking at her like she was an alien from Planet Nimrod. "What are you? A mutant ninja cockroach?"

"I had an audition and didn't have time to change before coming here." She looked down at her homemade costume then back up at the two men, battling her urge to scurry away like a crab avoiding the stewpot. She ignored Alex and held out her hand to Mr. Pickett. "Thanks for showing us around today."

"My pleasure." The attorney shook her hand while Alex turned away, dismissing her the same way he had all those years ago. She'd spent the year their parents had been married thinking the sun rose and fell because of him, and he'd seen her as nothing more than a nuisance. At least that's how it had felt back then. Now, she was a grown woman and refused to let him shove her aside. Too much depended on her being able to get her mother's affairs in order, and fast—her future, her career, her need to put this place behind her and move on.

"Let's get started then, shall we?" Mr. Pickett led them to the porch.

Alex followed first and Mandy trailed behind them, studying her ex-stepbrother more closely. He was still quarter-back handsome, with his black hair and chiseled features, his dark blue T-shirt and faded jeans clinging to his muscled bod. As they moved toward the house, though, she noticed a limp.

Huh. That was new.

Her pulse sped a bit and she opened her mouth to ask Alex how he'd hurt himself, but then Mr. Pickett unlocked the front door and gestured them inside, putting her questions on the back burner. Not that it was any of her business, but she was an actress. Studying people was research. That's the excuse she was going with, anyway.

"The house is livable," the attorney said, closing the door behind them. "But in need of some updates."

Mandy stepped around Alex and got her first peek at the interior. Much like the outside, it was well-worn and pretty basic. White walls, white ceiling, hardwood floors that needed a fresh buff. From the layer of dust and cobwebs, it looked like the place hadn't been occupied in a while. "No renters right now?"

"No, ma'am," Mr. Pickett said. "The last tenants moved out last year."

Her duffel bag slipped from her shoulder and plopped onto the floor at her feet, sending a small cloud of dust billowing. She coughed and waved her hand in front of her face. Mandy wasn't a fan of cleaning, but she'd kill for a mop right about now. This place would take more work to get it ready to sell than she'd first thought. Her hopes for a quick turnaround plummeted along with her heart, landing somewhere near her toes.

I'm trying to think positive, Mom. I'm really trying.

Alex stepped in beside her, the heat of his body at odds with the goose bumps on her chilly arms.

Mr. Pickett cleared his throat, then smiled politely as he switched on the lights. "Believe it or not, the house is listed on the national historic registry. With a little work, I think it would bring a tidy sum if you decide to sell."

"Who said anything about selling?" Alex inspected a piece of painted trim nearby, scraping off a chip with his nail. "This looks like mahogany. And I'd bet good money that plaster scrollwork on the ceiling is hand carved."

Mandy squinted up at the ceiling again and wondered how he could tell. His dad owned a construction company, so maybe Alex had some secret Spidey senses about building stuff. Not that it mattered. They wouldn't be keeping this place. "I can't maintain a house like this."

"I can," Alex said, following Mr. Pickett past a huge staircase with a carved banister and into a second room with more high ceilings and more designs in the plaster.

Sure, it was pretty enough, but it did nothing to stop the rising itch inside her. The longer she stood in this place, the more it felt like a trap. Her pulse kicked up another notch and her chest ached—not with grief this time, but with fear.

Fear that she'd get stuck in Heavenly Falls and never get to Hollywood. That was her dream—big lights, big city, big movie roles.

She took a deep breath and forced her tight shoulders to relax. Alex needed to see it was better to sell. That was all. Convincing people to believe what she wanted them to was what she did for a living. Shouldn't be that hard, right?

"How old is the house?" Alex asked the attorney, his words tinged with awe.

"The original blueprints from the county recorder's office say it was designed by Samuel and Joseph Cather Newsom in 1896."

"Seriously? This is a Newsom design?" Alex said at the same time Mandy said, "Wow, bound to be tons of problems with a house that old."

"It's a treasure." A muscle ticked near Alex's set jaw.

"It's a money pit." Mandy threw her hands up. "C'mon. You can't seriously be thinking of keeping this place."

"That's exactly what I'm thinking." He stepped closer, chest out and chin raised. "You don't have to be involved. I'll handle all the remodeling. And you can continue dressing up like bugs or germs or whatever it is you're supposed to be doing."

Cheeks burning and throat raw, she swallowed hard and clenched her hands at her sides. "What I'm supposed to be doing is honoring my mother's wishes and putting her estate to rest. And I've got as much stake in this place as you do, Alex Noonan, and I won't let you push me aside again."

She stepped forward, jabbing her index finger toward him.

"And, for the record, I'm an actress. A good one. I have a theater degree and everything. You don't like me being here any more than I do, but we're stuck in this together until we take care of this house, one way or another. Until then, I'm not going anywhere. Got it?"

He crossed his arms, his full lips forming a hard smile. "I'm not selling."

"Then I guess we're at an impasse." Mandy mirrored his defiant posture. She wasn't giving in, either. The proceeds from selling this house meant a big shot at stardom, a new chance at freedom, a chance to honor her mother's final wishes. No way would she give in to demands without a fight.

Mr. Pickett stood off to the side, fidgeting, as they faced off, gazes locked. Several long moments passed before Alex finally looked away, rubbing the back of his neck. "What if I buy you out?"

"You have the cash to do that?" She raised a brow at him. Back in the day, his family had money, but she had no idea what his current status was financially.

Alex cursed under his breath and shook his head, his big shoulders slumping. "Not yet."

He limped over to check out the fireplace mantel, and she released her pent-up breath. When he'd mentioned buying out her half, a lightbulb had lit in her head, only to be quickly extinguished. She glanced over at the attorney, who looked like he wanted to be anywhere but here. She knew the feeling. "Then I guess we're stuck with each other for a while."

Alex looked at her again, his dark eyes dull. "Guess so."

Mr. Pickett jumped into the conversation again. "Shall we continue the tour?"

They went down a wide hall to the kitchen at the back of the house. Again, it was serviceable but outdated and also needed a good scrub. Lime green painted cabinets hung on the walls and mismatched appliances dotted the room. In one corner sat a well-worn butcher block table with two chairs. Large windows graced the area above the sink, overlooking a fenced-in yard with a rose trellis. Early October meant the blooms were in decline, but Mandy imagined it would be pretty in the spring.

Beside her, Alex shuffled his feet then winced and rubbed his left thigh. Mandy couldn't resist asking, "What happened to your leg?"

"Accident," he grumbled, digging the toe of his boot into the black and white tiled floor.

"Working for your dad?"

"No." He turned away, swallowing hard. "For the IRS. As an investigator."

"Oh." She frowned. "I thought you planned to work for your dad after college."

"Well, I didn't." His sharp tone snapped through the quiet kitchen, and her heart flopped. He hurried after the attorney back out into the hall, saying over his shoulder, "Doesn't matter. It's all over now."

Uh-huh.

Small talk might not be her specialty, but Mandy was fluent in avoidance.

They toured a master bedroom with an attached bath then ended up back in the foyer. "There are more rooms on the second floor, but they haven't been used in some time.

"The third floor and attic are storage," Mr. Pickett said. "Any questions?"

"I'd still like to peek upstairs, if that's okay." She wanted a full picture of what she was in for with the place, however bad. Mandy grabbed ahold of the banister. "Be right back."

"Wait. I'm going, too." Alex moved toward the stairs, his limp more pronounced now. "Just be patient."

"Patience is my middle name." She tried for humor and failed miserably, if his skeptical look was any indication.

She'd thought maybe touring this place would take her mind off her grief, but she felt more drained than ever. Fatigue swelled inside her like a bruise as she followed Alex up the stairs, babbling to fill the awkward silence. "Actually, that's not true. My middle name is actually Prudence, after my maternal grandmother, but I don't spread that information around."

"I can see why. My condolences."

He'd quoted her favorite movie, *The Breakfast Club*.

The reminder brought another blast from the past to her tired brain—sitting with Alex and his siblings watching 80s teen rom-coms on repeat until they'd memorized all the lines. Alex had always made her special popcorn topped with Parmesan cheese and split Cherry Cokes with her. So sweet. Warm nostalgia took the edge off her irritation with him. Those had been good times.

Alex glanced back at her, his expression softer. "What was your audition for earlier?"

She snorted, glad for something to talk about besides the house situation. "Hand sanitizer." Mandy gestured toward her costume. "The casting director said I wasn't 'viral' enough."

They reached the upper landing and Alex turned to her with a small smile. One that highlighted those dimples in his cheeks. He'd been Mr. Popular when she'd been a kid, the guy all the other guys wanted to be and all the girls wanted to be with. He was different now, though. Everything was different.

Sadness scratched the back of her throat and she focused on the muted sunlight filtering in through the dusty windows.

"If it's any consolation, I think you look plenty contagious," he said, his frown returning. "Are you crying?"

"What? No." Annoyed with herself, Mandy swiped the back of her hand under her nose. "Dust."

"Sure." He didn't sound convinced, but they went in opposite directions before finally meeting up again at the top of the stairs. Given Alex's weird attachment to this place, and his lack of cash to buy her out, she needed a place to stay besides Gina's couch until she could get out of town.

The first floor wasn't bad and the second just needed a good cleaning. Since her own savings account was basically zilch at the moment, maybe living here in the short term was the most viable option.

Think positive. Better things are just around the corner.

Her fingers twitched at the thought of commitment, but determination steeled her spine. She could do this. She would do this. For her mother.

Get this place into shape, then get moving again.

Mandy wiped her damp palm on her striped tights, saying as much for herself as for him, "Fine."

"Fine what?" Alex tilted his head to the side.

"Fine, we both stay here and renovate this place before we decide how to proceed."

"Together?" The look on his face wavered between astonishment and apprehension before he gave a resigned sigh and said in a flat tone, "Fine."

They went back downstairs where Mr. Pickett waited by the front door. He handed them both a key to the house then withdrew an envelope from his pocket and gave it to Mandy. "Your mother asked that I deliver this today."

"What is it?" She reached for it with shaky fingers.

"No idea," the attorney said.

Mandy stared down at her name scrawled in her mother's handwriting on the outside of the envelope, heaviness settling over her once more.

The attorney started out the door, saying over his shoulder, "Good luck to you both."